On Stephen Baxter:

'Ideas come thick and fast, and an exhilarating sense of wonder is guaranteed' – *Independent*

'With every passing year, the oft-made remark that Baxter is Arthur C Clarke's heir seems more and more apt' – *SFX*

'There's real beauty and excitement to Baxter's writing' – *Starburst*

'Stephen Baxter is an incredibly skilled author – a successor to Arthur C Clarke and Philip K Dick...' – *Book Bag*

On Eric Brown:

'A masterful storyteller' – *Strange Horizons*

'Brown's spectacular creativity creates a constantly compelling read' – *Kirkus*

'SF infused with a cosmopolitan and literary sensibility... accomplished and affecting' – Paul J McAuley

'British writing with a deft, understated touch: wonderful' – *New Scientist*

THE spacetime PIT

plus two

STEPHEN**BAXTER**
ERIC**BROWN**

infinity plus

Published by infinity plus
www.infinityplus.co.uk
Follow @ipebooks on Twitter

ISBN-13: 978-0995752252
ISBN-10: 0995752257

CONTENTS

INTRODUCTION

by Eric Brown

COLLABORATION BETWEEN WRITERS IS a curious process.

I've tried writing with a number of authors, and it often doesn't work; there's no initial spark, or our writing styles, and methods, are too dissimilar to forge an effective working relationship. It doesn't matter how much I like the other person, or how similar our ideas about life, art and politics might be—if there isn't that elusive, almost alchemical spark at some point in the process, collaboration is doomed to a series of false starts and aborted stories.

My most prolific writing partner is Keith Brooke: together we've written more than a dozen stories, two novellas and a novel. With Keith, the process is wonderfully easy. What isn't so easy is finding the time to write something together: we live at opposite ends of the country, and for much of the time are often engaged on solo projects. On the rare occasions that our busy schedules afford us a window of opportunity, we swap ideas until something sparks, and not long after that we have a fully-fledged story-line, which one of us begins and then the other takes up, and so on, until the tale is finished.

The second writer I've collaborated with is the late Michael Coney, author of such classic SF novels as *Brontomek!*, *Hello Summer, Goodbye*, and *The Girl With A Symphony In Her Fingers*, as well as a host of excellent short stories. Although we lived half a world apart at the time, Mike in British Columbia and I in England, we corresponded by email and over a period of six months wrote a long short story, the biological murder-mystery set on an alien world, 'The Trees of Terpsichore Three', which was published in the Scottish SF magazine *Spectrum 8*.

I've also collaborated with my friend and fellow curry aficionado Tony Ballantyne, author the Hard SF novels *Recursion* and *Twisted Metal*, and one of my favourite fantasy novels of all time, *Dream London*. A while back I wrote a series of stories about a race of aliens who come to Earth and bestow the gift of voluntary immortality on the human race. Tony liked these tales, and had an idea for one. He started the story, I took it up and finished it, and then we each rewrote the other's sections. 'Matthew's Passion', collected in my fix-up novel *Kéthani*, is the result: Tony imbued the tale with spirituality and his knowledge of music, attributes I signally lack.

Which brings me to the collaborations which form the content of the current volume, *The Spacetime Pit Plus Two,* and my collaborator, Stephen Baxter, the author of such ground-breaking novels as *The Time-Ships, Evolution, The Light of Other Days* with Arthur C Clarke, and the Xeelee story sequence.

I first met Steve at a science-fiction convention, the Nottingham MexiCon of 1989. We'd both just started selling short stories to markets such as *Interzone* and David S Garnett's *Zenith* anthologies, and were in the process of writing our first novels. Not only did we have our writing in common, and our love of the genre, but a passion for football: Steve follows Liverpool, while I, for my sins, suffer the travails of Leeds United. We got on well, and it wasn't long before one of us suggested collaborating on a story or two.

This was over twenty years ago, and sad to say I have no recollection of how we went about the process of collaboration, though Steve reminds me that we worked on 'Spacetime...' when I visited him in Prestwood in the summer of '95. I do recall that I had the initial idea for 'The Spacetime Pit', which Steve, with his scientific and technological nous, proceeded to pull apart at the seams and stitch back together in a way that would work. It's a grim tale that spans billions of years, but has the dilemma of a human being at its very core. 'Spacetime...' won the 1996 *Interzone* readers' poll for best story.

The second story in the volume is 'Green-Eyed Monster'. By contrast, it's a light-hearted tale about bodily transmogrification, love and jealousy. It's nice to be able to write a tale from the viewpoint of a toad from time to time. I rarely write humorous stories, but on rereading this one I found myself chuckling: Steve must have written those passages.

The final story, 'Sunfly', is a strange tale set on a very alien world—a strip of land girdling a sun—and follows the exploits of student Onara as she comes to understand not only her world but her destiny within its complex history.

Enough. Herein, collected for the first time in one volume for your entertainment, is *The Spacetime Pit Plus Two...*

Eric Brown
Cockburnspath
January 2018

THE SPACETIME PIT

SHUTTLE LURCHED. "PRIMARY shipboard systems failure."

Wake stared through the monitor as lightning leapt between fat cotton-wool clouds. She was deep inside this remote gravity well, *inside* a storm, and fast falling further in.

"Switch to secondary, Shuttle. Affirm."

Shuttle bucked through turbulent air.

"I said, 'Affirm.'"

"Crew loss scenario."

She felt sweat prickle her skin beneath her flight suit. "Detail."

"Ninety per cent likelihood of secondary shipboard systems failure."

Shit. That was non-survivable, all right, according to the book.

"Switch to manual. Tell Mother I'm aborting the landing and coming home."

"Boosters inoperable. No pressure in propellant tank. Crew loss—"

"—scenario. Right," she muttered. *Now what?*

Shuttle was old, but it wasn't supposed to fail. It was loaded up with redundant systems to keep it functioning, if minimally, for years.

In the end, though, everything failed. If it hadn't been this storm, the lightning strikes Shuttle had taken, it would have been some other damn thing, on some other remote world.

Wake was on her own, out here at the rim of human expansion. Her training had hammered home that, in the end, she couldn't rely on the equipment. It was up to her to keep herself alive. *If A fails, try B! If B fails, try C!*

If she couldn't get back to orbit, she'd land. She would need raw materials, for repairs, fuel. She couldn't see the surface, had no real idea what kind of conditions she was dropping into here. She'd have to deal with that later.

Lightning leapt before Shuttle, flashing in Wake's face, dazzling her. Shuttle took a sickening dive to starboard.

"Give me the coordinates of the Alpha One landmass."

"Affirm."

The grey, ragged clouds parted, revealing an ocean of beaten grey steel. On the horizon sat an island, mountainous, irregular. She was skimming just a couple of hundred metres above peaking waves.

Christ. And it's only an hour since I was in the sauna on Mother.

"Secondary systems shutdown imminent."

"Advise emergency procedure."

"Crew loss scenario."

"Oh, for God's sake—"

Shuttle was now, frankly, falling out of the sky. *One option left.* She got out of her seat and staggered towards Pod. Shuttle's floor tipped under her in a compound, violent motion; she lurched, clattering against consoles and equipment boxes.

She reached the long, hexagonal coffin and slid inside. Cold subdermals snaked over her skin.

"Instructions," Pod said.

"Use your heuristic algorithms. Assess the situation. Ensure minimal danger. Prepare damage reports, locality surveys, survival scenarios…"

"Affirm."

The lid closed over her. She closed her hands over the locket at her neck and thought of Ben.

She felt a kick in the back as Pod threw itself out of Shuttle.

SHE'D ORBITED THE fifth planet of this dim star, a hundred light years from Earth, for two days, before deciding to come in for a closer look. It looked vaguely Earthlike: thick cloud cover over transparent oxygen-nitrogen air, oceans of water. The only landmass of any significance was the largest island of an archipelago straddling the equator. There were traces of green on the island, but her sensors didn't betray any hint of chlorophyll. She couldn't see any sign of Eetee organisation—no industrial smog, no large structures, no radio or other signals.

She was pretty sure the planet wouldn't be directly habitable, and there would be no Contact here. But maybe it could be terraformed.

Wake was paid by a complicated system to do with the number of useful worlds she turned up in each survey sweep, and how useful each world was. *Possibly terraformable* was pretty low down the list of desirables and wouldn't pay her much.

Maybe just enough to justify a landing, she'd decided at last.

The day after this landing, she'd been due to ship out and head home. In fact she was only three days from Earth, using Mother's Alcubierre FTL drive.

SHE SURFACED THROUGH a sea of anaesthetics.

"Status report."

"Crew survival not assured."

Terrific. She struggled to sit up. Pod was tilted, so her head was maybe twenty degrees below her feet, and the crystal canopy was obscured by something—the drapes of the parachute, she realised belatedly. Through the uncovered half of the canopy she made out a blindingly green-blue sky.

Green? Of course. From the scattering of the orange light of this G8-class sun—

"Where's Mother?"

"Orbital elements are one hundred twenty-three point four by–"

"Show me."

Fine reticles appeared in the glass of the canopy. Guided by them she picked out a silver point steady in the south-west sky, brilliant despite the daylight: Mother, in its stationary orbit, over this landmass. She felt a surge of relief.

Pod's report said the air outside was close enough to Earth's to sustain her for a few hours, but there were some mild toxins. She could spend no more than a couple of hours at a time out of Pod. She couldn't move far, then.

Temperature thirty Celsius. *A bright summer's day on Alpha One.*

Right now Mother would be sending out 'Crew Loss' buoys. If Wake could get to Shuttle she could instruct Mother to start emitting mayday FTL buoys, telling the Universe she was still alive. There was no guarantee anyone would respond, but it was a better chance than nothing.

And if she did get to Shuttle, of course, she might do better than that; maybe she could figure out a way to get back to orbit, to Mother.

She pushed at the canopy; it opened with a sigh of hydraulics, shrugging off the parachute.

Pod had come down in the foothills of an eroded mountain range. She stood on a grass-covered plateau.

Well, it looks like grass. Beyond the lip of the plateau a green valley fell away, widening towards a ribbon of ocean to the south. A quicksilver thread of river twisted across the valley bottom. *U-shaped valley. Glaciated, probably.* There were plants, something like trees: short, thick-boled, with a haze of crimson leaves. The sun sat on the horizon, huge, too orange.

The panorama was sufficiently *different* to send a shiver down her spine.

She touched the locket around her neck. From within the heart-shaped crystal Ben smiled. Ben's two girls— Wake's granddaughters, microgravity-slender—held onto his arm and waved. The hologram had been taken in the Shelter, the big, bright, grass-walled chamber at the heart of the L5 colony, the place children were brought up. The Earth colours, the chlorophyll green of the grass and trees, were strikingly different from Alpha One. As if this planet was a poor mock-up.

She kneeled down and picked a few blades of the 'grass'. It was more like a six-fold clover leaf. And the green tint was like copper oxide, not chlorophyll-bright.

"Pod. Tell me about the biota."

"Most numerous atoms are silicon, hydrogen, oxygen. Silicon bonds form the basic architecture of—"

She stopped listening. *Oh, great. I've discovered silicon-based life.* That was supposed to be impossible. Silicon couldn't form double bonds like carbon; silicon couldn't form the metastable compounds which encouraged the development of large, complex molecules... Evidently, nature here had found a way.

It didn't matter a damn to her. Basic science was part of her contract, but it paid hardly anything. What was most significant was the fact that not even Pod's smart digestive sacs would be able to turn these silicon-based raw materials into food for her.

She interrupted Pod's lecture. "Tell me about supplies."

"Five days at nominal intake."

Five days of gloop fed to her intravenously by the sub-dermals. *I need to find that damn Shuttle.*

Pod gave her a bearing for Shuttle's crash site. It was a kilometre to the south, down the valley.

She walked over soft, grass-carpeted ground, plucking diamond-shaped leaves from the trees. The green wasn't quite right, and neither was the sky, but it was almost impossible to believe that there was nothing here she could eat.

The crash site was a scar in the hillside, all but grown over. She found what might have been the comms deck; its case was corroded and broken open, and a kind of lichen spilled out when she tried to lift it.

She went back to Pod. "How long have I been down here?"

"Two local years." Which was about one Earth year.

"A *year?* Why so long?"

"Pod seeking crew survival assurance. Not attainable. Opened at limit of heuristic algorithms for further direction."

She squatted down on the grass and hugged her knees. She hadn't anticipated such a gap. She hadn't even thought to ask Pod how long she'd been inert. *Too damn long*; so long she'd already lost Shuttle, in the accelerated entropy of this spacetime pit.

She figured options.

She could try to signal. But, hell, she didn't have enough power to send anything that would be picked up at interstellar distances. And besides, it would take decades for a lightspeed signal to reach anywhere inhabited.

She could try to build a Shuttle, get back to orbit. Yeah. But she knew Pod didn't have the resources to enable her to turn unmined iron ore into a spacegoing craft. And besides, she was no engineer.

She was trapped here, in this gravity pit, alone, out of touch, and everybody who knew her must have been told she was dead.

She let go, just for a second.

Then she straightened up. *To hell with that.* She needed some options.

...At the foot of the valley, two or three kilometres away, a thin thread of smoke rose into the air.

SHE HURRIED BACK to Pod. She slipped a vocoder headset over her head, fixing the microphone before her mouth, and then she fastened a laser pistol to her belt.

The sun had climbed from the horizon. *It's local morning, then.* Another thing she hadn't thought to inquire of Pod. *I have to get more observant, less self-obsessed, if I'm to live through this.* She walked down the steep hillside into the valley.

There were fields in the valley bottom. They were delimited by low walls of boulders, glacial deposit hauled away from the soil. She made out more threads of smoke, a collection of tiny, mud-coloured huts. *Eetees.*

She passed small brown quadrupeds: ruminants browsing on the grass-analogue. Silicon-based birds pulsed through the air around her, their chirps high and piercing. The whole place was just a feast of convergent evolution, she thought.

After a kilometre she found a path worn into the hillside. She followed the twisting, copper-coloured track to the valley bottom.

The first dwelling she came to, a timber and adobe shack on stilts, was on the other side of a field planted with orderly rows of what looked like beet. There were crude ploughs, made of some wood-analogue, standing around in the field. *Not technologically advanced, then.* This could be the sticks, of course. She needed to find a city, industrial advancement.

She was forming a tentative plan. It would take the resources of a partially industrialised society, at least, to project her back to orbit. Maybe these Eetees had space technology. If so, she had to find it.

It wasn't a good plan, but it was all she had.

There was movement in the field before her.

The Eetee was kneeling beside a row of the beet stuff, facing away from her. It straightened, and stared up into the empty sky.

Reptile, she thought immediately: specifically, a frog. A silicon-based frog. The thing was bilaterally symmetric: two arms, two legs. Its portly torso stood on spindly legs; its skin colour was a lustrous brown, almost as if lacquered. It wore a length of dun cloth over its loins area. Modesty? A tool belt?

The Eetee turned around. Its domed head was even more frog-like: two bulbous eyes, a wide slit of a mouth— but the eyes were sheltered *under* the mouth. It looked as if its head was upside down. Its naked chest was patterned with three mustard-yellow chevrons.

When its gaze met Wake's, it froze, staring at her.

Slowly she raised her hand in salute. Any tool-making biped ought to respond to the gesture. Wake crossed the field, between the rows of leafy plants. Two metres from the Eetee she started to speak, making random greetings.

The Eetee was small, barely reaching her midriff. Its yellow eyes triangulated on her face. The Eetee issued a series of sibilant burbles. After a couple of minutes the vocoder blipped.

"...my field? What do you want? Have you come to damage the crops? What..."

"I am a traveller. My name is Katerina Wake." She pointed to herself. "And you?"

The Eetee peered up from under its mouth, listening to words that weren't synchronised with her oddly-placed lips. "I am a planter and grower of crops. I am—" A gurgle. The vocoder projected a transliteration onto her eyeball. "F'han Lha."

"What do you call your people?"

It just looked back at her.

That was a bad sign. A lack of a name to distinguish the locals meant the Eetee didn't know of anyone beyond its immediate group. Even in theory. And if this Eetee thought that this squalid little community contained the only people in the world, there couldn't be much in the way of travel, trade, communication.

Not likely to be any spaceships, either. I've landed in a silicon-based Middle Ages.

F'han's gaze dropped from Wake's face and regarded the locket at her neck. She pulled the locket over her head and held it before the Eetee's fascinated eyes, let the hologram cycle.

F'han reached out with three-fingered hands. No opposable thumb, she noticed.

"For me?"

"No. I'm sorry." She slipped the locket back over her neck.

Three more Eetees came clambering down a ladder in the underside of the stilted hut. They loped towards her, their gait low and regular. "F'han!"

F'han ran through the field towards the others. The newcomers must have been as tall as Wake; one of them clutched F'han's head protectively. *I've been talking to a child.*

Quickly, the four Eetees climbed the rickety wood-analogue ladder and disappeared into the dark underside of the dwelling.

SHE WALKED BACK up the valley wall to Pod.

She could stretch Pod's supplies to ten or fifteen days by going to half-rations. And she could always spin out her time on the surface by going back into stasis, inside Pod. Pod was self-maintaining. She could last down here for months, years, if she had to, living a few hours at a time… But for what? So she could starve next year instead of this?

Of course F'han was only a kid. It wouldn't know everything. Maybe there was a glittering city just beyond the hills… But she would have seen it from orbit. *Face it, Wake. This is all there is. Silicon-based subsistence farmers: nothing more or less.*

These Eetees had to be generations away from developing a technology sufficient to help her: to sustain her complex biochemical needs, to lift her back to orbit.

If A fails, try B! If B fails, try C!…

Well, if the Eetees couldn't help her *now*, she'd just have to wait until they could. She'd climb into Pod and wait it out as long as was necessary for these Eetees to scratch their way to some kind of technology; she could hold out a hell of a long time, in Pod.

Into the face of the rock behind Pod she lasered a low crevice, and then, over the next hour, she pushed Pod into the narrow overhang. She banked up earth and rock against the length of Pod; now it would be protected from the weather, and, when the grass-analogue grew on the earthworks, hidden from easy observation.

She climbed into Pod.

"Instructions?"

How long? She needed to wait out enough time to see if the Eetees were on an upwards technological curve, or not. But not so long that she stranded herself out of time.

Fifty years?

In fifty years, Ben would probably be dead. And the girls would be middle-aged women—as old as Wake was now. She found it hard to accept that in subjective seconds the people she loved most would have lived their lives without her.

But she didn't have a lot of choice, she thought bleakly.

"Fifty years. Earth standard."

She closed her eyes, and submitted to the embrace of the subdermals.

SHE AWOKE, AND lay there waiting for the lid to open.

She felt no different, as if she'd barely closed her eyes. She left Pod and pushed through the soil and undergrowth. The sky looked unchanged. To the south west she could see Mother, a spark of light unmoving in the green-blue sky.

She put on the vocoder and made her way down the valley. She took a footpath across a fallow field towards the farm where, fifty years ago, she'd spoken with F'han Lha.

A group of Eetees laboured in their stony fields. The spindly-limbed frog people had their wood-analogue ploughs shackled to their backs, and they scraped furrows through the crimson earth. The workers looked up, observed her progress for a few seconds, then returned incuriously to their toil.

More labourers were standing in line by the silver river. As Wake watched, they passed containers fashioned from gourds along the line. The last workers tipped the water onto the earth. It was laborious, fantastically inefficient.

She could see no signs of change.

She felt a sharp contempt for the Eetees. For how many centuries had they lived like this, enduring their bucolic existence of birth, work in the fields, death?

The orange sun beat down on her head; she was hot, ragged, hungry, alone. *So much for my plan.* Well, then, she thought with a trace of angry desperation, she would just have to tip the damn Eetees out of their dull, comfortable equilibrium.

She went to stand in the shade of the stilted farmhouse, and waited.

What she was planning wasn't exactly ethical. But ethics, for a mankind spreading desperately across new planets, were a luxury.

Ethical behaviour wasn't even in her training.

WHEN THE SUN got to its highest point, the workers trudged from the fields and the river. They shaded themselves under the farmhouse, and pushed mashed beet into the mouths on the tops of their skulls.

Wake stood before them. As the Eetees ate, they watched her blankly. "Where I come from we do things differently. Better. Easier." She picked up a sharp rock and began to scratch a crude diagram into the wood-analogue panels of the farmhouse. It was a tube curled into a spiral, around a central cylinder. If the diagram didn't work she'd make a couple of simple models.

One of the Eetees came closer, apparently curious, a tall, wispy individual with a ring of green spots on its carapace.

"We draw water with this. It is easier. This device is called an Archimedes screw…"

"INSTRUCTIONS."

She kissed the locket. "I'm sorry, Ben."

She was sliding deeper into this pit in space and time. But what choice was there? *I'm falling in, because there's nothing I can hold onto...*

This is one hell of a plan, Wake.

"Instructions," Pod repeated.

She closed her eyes. "Two hundred years. Earth standard." Maybe that would be long enough for the seed she'd planted to bear fruit.

If A fails, try B! If B fails, try C!...

SHE OPENED HER eyes. Above her, the crystal cover was cracked.

She pushed open the canopy and climbed out. She was stiff, her limbs sore, her stomach constricted. It was night; the clouds above her head were thick, rain-laden, and a sulphur yellow glow illuminated their undersides.

Change, she thought immediately, and she exulted.

Her earthwork was gone, and Pod had been dragged out of its crevice and set on an apron of stone cobbles, surrounded by tall iron railings. Along Pod's silver flank there were scrapes and dents; it looked as if someone had tried to prise open the canopy.

Her heart beat faster. *I've induced curiosity, then.*

She crossed the cobbles, gripped the railings and peered through. She was still in the foothills—the worn mountains loomed behind her, dark, deserted—and to the south the valley, faintly outlined, fell away beyond this little compound. But now artificial lights glowed across the valley, in tight yellow splashes. She saw that roadways criss-crossed what had been a wide green plain. Stone dwellings filled the valley bottom, clustered about dark, oppressive buildings: mills, factories perhaps. The river had been straightened out, dammed; huge spiral devices that she recognised as remote descendants of her Archimedes screw lined the engineered valley, pumping water into rectilinear irrigation ditches. At the mouth of the valley, remote, she saw the lights of a town, densely-packed streets, smog-laden air.

Through the hazy air she could just see a crude harbour at the edge of the ocean beyond.

She gazed into the south west sky, looking for Mother. But the clouds were thick, and a haze of smog hung over the valley.

"…Halt! Do not move."

The command, with Eetee sibilants overlaid by her vocoder's whisper, came from behind her. She raised her hands in the air, showing them empty.

"Turn. Slowly."

Again, she obeyed.

Two solid-looking Eetees, garbed in black, tight uniforms, stood outside the Pod compound. They were covering her with what looked like crossbows. She could see the bolts; they were sharp, massive and grooved with a spiral rifling. Evidently, she thought wryly, her Archimedes-screw revolution had had a few unexpected spin-offs.

One of the Eetees opened a heavy gate and entered the compound. It raised its inverted head and glared at her with golden eyes. Then it crossed to Pod, and peered through the closed crystal canopy. It hissed something at its companion, too fast for the vocoder, then left the compound and started working at a squat machine at the brow of the valley. She heard the crackle of electricity. From the machine, sulphurous light glared out over the valley, in a dot-dash sequence. *A signal. They've been watching, waiting for me to emerge. And now that I have, they're signalling.*

After that, they waited. The Eetees wouldn't let her return to Pod, so she sat down on the cobbles, miming weariness.

After half an hour a growling rumble came up out of the valley. She stood, and the Eetees let her come to the railings.

A squat steam-truck was climbing the wall of the valley. Two Eetees in glittering ponchos sat on its roof, grandly, before a pair of funnels which spouted steam. The wheels were big, wood-spoked, iron-rimmed. Whatever boiler was hidden inside the boxy frame of the vehicle wasn't strong enough to haul the truck up the hill, and there was a crude harness arrangement in front of the truck. A dozen or more Eetees were strapped into the harness, dragging at the truck as it bumped over the uneven ground. A serf looked up at her vaguely, its mouth gaping open. It had a mustard yellow chevron on its bare chest, and—she was astonished to see—a crude locket, carved from wood, around its neck. The locket was obviously a clumsy imitation of her own. Perhaps, then, the serf was a descendant of F'han Lha; could the memory of her last brief emergence have been passed down the generations?

The two Eetees on top looked fat, sleek and well-dressed. The harnessed serfs, by comparison, appeared scrawny, exhausted, bruised.

You've become a serpent in paradise, Wake, she thought.

The truck pulled up in front of the railings.

Two serfs helped one of the riding Eetees down to the ground. It approached Wake, waddling imperiously. Its poncho glowed crimson with copper inlays. She saw that its upper carapace had a marking, a circle of green dots, and it wore a pendant of its own, in the shape of an Archimedes spiral.

She felt overwhelmed. These people must have been ready for stimulation. Receptive. They'd taken the fragments she'd given them and built whole subcultures; she felt as if aspects of her personality were being reflected back at her, extrapolated to absurd lengths.

She held her hands out, palm up, questioning. "What do you want?"

The Eetee pointed to her vocoder, her clothes, Pod. It said something; it was a crude attempt to pronounce 'Archimedes'.

She was starting to feel breathless; already she needed to get back to Pod. Damn it. There just wasn't *time* to think any of this through.

These people did not appear motivated to help her. They just wanted what she had. She had to find out if they were a positive threat.

She pointed at Pod. "Mine," she said bluntly. "Not yours."

The serfs, still strapped into their brutal harnesses, stirred at this. She was hardly an expert at Eetee body language, but it seemed to her they were finding some kind of inspiration in her words of defiance. *Interesting.* Maybe there was an angle there she could exploit.

Green-Ring gestured. A soldier type raised its spiral crossbow and aimed at her head.

Wake's heart hammered, and she felt saliva pool at the back of her throat. *So. A threat, indeed. What now, Wake?*

She had to adjust their attitude. *Make them focus on a goal we can all share.*

She said, "Key. For Pod—for my tomb." She held her hands up, and started to lower them slowly towards her belt, to the laser pistol there.

Green-Ring seemed to be hesitating. She could see the soldiers' triple fingers tightening around their crossbow triggers.

She got the pistol out. She held it up for them to see, gambling they wouldn't recognise it as a weapon. "Key. Okay?"

She turned, holding the pistol up above her head, and started to walk back to Pod.

Then, with one movement, she turned and thumbed the laser's power switch. A wand of red light, intense in the smoggy gloom, arced over her head, supernaturally straight. Before the Eetees could move she brought the beam slicing down over a soldier, neatly lopping away an arm. Its crossbow clattered to the ground.

The soldier stared down at the stump, which was pumping out some dark blood-analogue. Then it fell backwards, its eyes rolling up, its remaining limbs in spasm.

She advanced on the Eetees. She held up the locket and let the hologram cycle, glittering Earth green and blue. "Hear me! I will return in–" she calculated quickly "–one hundred years. Then, I will give you, your children, this light, the contents of my tomb. But in return..." She stabbed the wand of light at the clouds. "In return, you will build a machine to lift me into the sky. Take me to the light which orbits." The vocoder couldn't translate that. "The star which shines, steady in the sky." Enough. They had generations to figure it out. "Do it, or I will call down more light from the sky, and destroy your fields and factories, and turn the rivers and seas to steam, and cut your children to small pieces..."

The serfs—the descendants of the peasant-boy F'han, maybe—were shouting at her now, waving their arms in the air, holding up their crudely carved copies of her locket. *Good grief,* she thought. *They think I'm a god.* She hadn't anticipated that. Would it help, or harm her?

This culture, this valley world, was like a tub of paraffin into which, periodically, she was throwing lighted matches. She couldn't predict how this was going to turn out, if this latest absurd gamble would pay off.

It was too late to do anything about it.

She turned her back and walked to Pod, stiffly, expecting a crossbow bolt between her shoulder blades at each step.

She accepted the embrace of the sub-dermals with relief.

POD SHOOK; MUFFLED booms reached her cocooned cabin.

Beyond the canopy's starred glass there was a flare of light. Lightning? No, it burned orange red.

Like aircraft fuel.

She pushed open the canopy and sat up; she felt old, stiff, beaten up.

The sky was huge, aquamarine, clear again. She located Mother, a spark of light in its south west station, sailing serene above it all. But the sky was marred by contrails, white puffs of explosions, remote bangs.

The ancient hills still rose behind her, but something about them was different: in several places their profile had been altered, notched. In one place she saw the distant glint of glass, of fused rock.

She walked to the lip of the valley. The cobbled pavement was cratered rubble, the railings a tangle of rusting iron. There was an extensive barricade around Pod's enclosure now: earthworks, and what looked like tank traps.

The earthworks extended down into the valley bottom: miles of them, bristling with gun emplacements and something like barbed wire.

Bedraggled Eetee soldiers moved through the mud. She saw several injured: stumps of amputated limbs, crudely bandaged carapaces. Many of the wounds looked infected. Evidently medical science hadn't advanced as much as the art of war.

Beyond the earthworks the valley was desolated, the ground smashed, the small trees reduced to burned stumps. The port town she remembered in the distance had been flattened, reduced to a rectilinear grid of foundations. Fires burned, unattended, and she thought she could see ragged Eetees picking their way through rubble. The smog was gone, though. This war must have dragged on for years; there could have been no industry in this valley for a long time. Now, she could easily see all the way to the coast...

And there she made out a row of gantries, stark and grey, and at each there was a slender spire, glowing pearl white in the sun, wreathed with vapour.

Her breath caught. *More convergent evolution.* It might have been Canaveral or Tyuratam, Mergui or Tanega Shima: any of Earth's spaceports. *It worked, by God. They are preparing to loft me to orbit.*

A few hundred yards below her, a soldier in the earthworks spotted her. It started jabbering to its companions. More of them poked their carapaced heads above the trenches, and shouted. Then they began to clamber out, some of them awkward on injured limbs, and came towards her. Most of them were wearing amulets around their necks, and they held them up, aping the gesture she'd made yesterday... or fifty Earth standard years before.

They began to chant, and the vocoder whispered. *I will call down light from the sky. I will destroy your fields and factories, and turn the rivers and seas to steam, and cut your children to small pieces...* They were gathering into a mob, and climbing the slope towards her.

She backed off, making sure she had a way back to Pod. So her scheme had worked. It was obvious these people worshipped her, to some degree; in fact they were defending Pod's site. *(From who?)* Maybe these were the descendants of the oppressed serfs she'd seen last time. Maybe, inspired by her memory, they'd thrown off their masters.

And this was their millennium: the second coming she had predicted, and was now fulfilling.

Right now, she was scared of being worshipped to death. And for all their fervour these people weren't much use to her anyhow. She had to get to that coastal launch complex...

The ground shuddered. Cobbles exploded into the air. She threw herself to the ground and covered her head with her arms; the Eetee troops fell back, screaming.

What now? Artillery? But she'd seen no flash, or smoke, and surely she would have heard any incoming projectile. A quake, then?

The shuddering went on and on. Smashed paving hailed down around her.

The ground broke open, not ten feet away. A metal snout shoved upwards, out of the earth, gleaming silver, spinning with a whine of worn bearings. The craft hauled its way out of its pit, laboriously, and tipped forward onto the surface. It was a fat cylinder with a spiral screw blade wrapped around its hull, like an Archimedes screw writ large and lethal. The blade stopped turning, and round hatches in the flanks of the craft tipped outwards. Troops spilled out of the steaming metal hull, shouting, bearing heavy rifles; they wore copper-coloured ponchos strapped tightly to their bodies, laden with ammunition and other equipment.

So the oppressing class is still around. In fact it made sense; it must be the 'oppressors', more technically advanced than the soldiers in the trenches, who had developed that launch complex.

She got to her feet. The siege-busting Eetees spotted her immediately; they pointed and shouted.

Her mind whirled. Should she throw in her lot with these poncho types, let them take her to the launch complex on the coast?

But they didn't look all that friendly. She remembered the naked greed of Green-Ring. These people evidently didn't venerate her; they just wanted what she had. And, despite the existence of that launch complex, they might be prepared to rob her without fulfilling their half of their bargain. At least the serfs were trying to protect her.

What do I do? Which side do I pick?

There was a growl from the trenches beyond the lip of the plateau. The ponchos turned, raising their weapons. A broad iron muzzle poked over the lip; huge tracked wheels sent earth spraying across the smashed cobbles. It was some kind of primitive tank, venting steam from a row of stacks, climbing up from the trenchworks. Behind it, serf trench troops were clambering onto the cobbled platform, shouting and waving their weapons.

The muzzle of the tank's main gun swivelled to point at the earth burrower, and the ponchos ran forward to engage the trench troops. The burrower's spiral screw began to spin, as if it was trying to get away.

It was all happening too quickly for Wake. *When in doubt, follow your gut.*

She made her choice. She ran forward, reaching for the burrower's closing hatches.

Before she got to the burrower, light flashed from the coast, dazzling, white and orange. Wake threw herself to the ground once more. The tank, the battling troops, were thrown into grotesque silhouette.

The noise arrived then, an immense clatter, so violent it rattled her chest cavity.

She lifted up her face. *Rocket light.* She stood up and shoved her way forward, past the dazzled, mesmerised troops, to the lip of the plateau.

The rockets on the coast had been launched. White smoke billowed in great plumes from the launch pads. She counted three, four, five of the slim white needles, thrusting towards the greenish sky on droplets of intense yellow light.

She felt panic clutch at her chest. *Too early! They launched too early! I'm not aboard, damn it!*

Then she looked more closely. The rising rockets were of a crude design: mostly fuel tank, with a small cone for payload at the tip. Too small to carry a human, or an Eetee.

They weren't spaceships, she realised. They were missiles.

It was impossible to be sure with the naked eye, but it looked as if they were climbing up to meet Mother, the bright, steady star in the south west.

The pieces fell into place quickly. *These ponchos had no intention of helping me. They want to destroy Mother. So I won't be able to bring down fire on their children, as I threatened... And when Mother's gone, they'll come for me.*

One hell of a plan, Wake.

But these primitives surely couldn't damage Mother, even if the missiles reached their target.

She thought of the notched hills, the glassy crater.

Nukes. They have nukes. And they've used them already.

Mother couldn't survive a nuclear attack.

Mother was powered by a colour-force drive: chromodynamics, the strong nuclear force. An order of magnitude more energy-dense than the weak forces involved in fission explosions. If the Eetees managed to disrupt Mother's hull, if the colour drive went up, then this damn planet would be wiped clean.

The nuclear-tipped missiles had almost risen out of sight. She turned and ran to Pod. It was the only place she might be safe.

The bands of Eetees, their shock at the launches fading, had started to wade into each other once again. Some of them broke off to chase after her. The burrower was pulling itself back into its pit in the ground.

She threw herself into Pod and dragged shut the canopy. Eetees clustered around Pod, hammering on the starred and scuffed surface.

"Instructions."

"Heuristic algorithms," she said quickly.

Distorted frog faces pressed up against the crystal canopy. The sub-dermals embraced her.

A light blossomed above her, far brighter than the sun.

Thumbless hands scrabbled at the canopy, leaving trails of slime that blistered and burned dry.

Then even the shadows were burned away, and she was enfolded in light.

THE LID LIFTED. Sunlight, bright orange, flooded Pod's interior, but a deep cold worked into her bones.

Wake pushed herself up. She felt weak, fragile. She pulled at the cloth of her flight suit; pieces of it came away in her fingers. *Rotted.*

She stood up. She had to stand still, as the sky spun around her. She felt as if she had been out for…

How long?

She stepped out of Pod. The sun hung in an empty, washed-out, green-blue sky, shedding no heat. No contrails.

No Mother.

Some of the floor cobbles survived, but they were smashed, eroded smooth as pebbles. No grass-analogue grew between them. Ice coated the exposed earth. There was ash, soot, mixed in with the ice, little grains of it.

She walked to the lip of the plateau. The atmosphere was thin, as if she was at high altitude; her lungs strained, trying to extract oxygen from the cold air.

The valley was a sculpture in white and brown. Here and there rock, fused and glassy, protruded through the compacted snow. It looked as if a glacier was forming here. There was no grass, no trees. Nothing moved. No bird sang. She could see no sign of the scar in the hillside left by Shuttle's crash.

She shielded her stinging eyes and looked out to the coast. The town was gone, the harbour. There was an angular form that looked like the stump of one of the launch gantries. Huge icicles dangled from it. On the sea, white glinted. Bergs.

The cold was astonishing.

She was gasping. The oxygen content was way down on what she'd observed before. She returned to Pod and pulled out an air mask, fitted it over her face. "Atmospheric content," she said to Pod. "Interpretation."

"Combustion of biota. Global. Free oxygen removed."

"But no replenishment?"

"Not observed. Oxygen levels continue to decline. Crew survival not assured."

"How long was I out?"

"Forty-two thousand, five hundred and–"

Jesus. Tens of millennia.

Long enough for the radioactive products of that last nuclear war and Mother's destruction to decay to harmlessness. Long enough for the ash of the burned biosphere to fall to the ground in rain and, later, snow; long enough for the ruined planet to tip to a new climatic equilibrium: permanent winter, coated with ice, reflecting most of the sun's heat back to space.

Nothing left alive. I've killed the children of F'han Lha. I've even killed the forests and the algae and the plankton, or whatever silicon-based equivalent used to pump oxygen into this air.

Crew survival not assured, indeed.

She still had the locket around her neck. She took hold of the little pendant, held it up, turned it. It was dark. The hologram had failed, its tiny internal battery emptied.

She grieved.

Now what?

The random thought made her laugh, gasping into the mask.

I've stranded myself in this spacetime pit: a hundred light years from home, and forty thousand years out of my time. Longer than my species existed on Earth, before my own birth.

Now here's my plan.

ACTUALLY, SHE DISCOVERED after a while, she *did* have a plan.

Of course it was absurd. But the alternative was to give up.

SHE SPENT A day of consciousness, a whole precious day, working through her scheme.

She dug a hole in the frozen ground with her laser. She buried a heater in the permafrost, and stretched a power line between the heater and Pod.

She cannibalised Pod's digestive sac. She set it to process the inert soil into amino acids, nucleotide bases, sugars: aminos for proteins, bases and sugars for nucleic acids, the building blocks of terrestrial life.

She took a sample of her own stomach bacteria and stored it cryogenically. She set the capsule to release gut bacteria samples, at timed intervals.

Her scheme was simple, elemental. She would propagate terrestrial life on this planet.

She'd nurture life, for as long as it took, and repopulate the world. Next time she climbed out of Pod there should be carbon-based biomass that Pod could process to feed her.

It was a fine plan. All she had to do was create life, evolve a sentient race, and educate them to take her home: whatever she might find there, anyhow, after forty millennia.

Simple. *If A fails, try B! If B fails, try C!*

While the machinery was setting up, she sat on the frozen ground, her knees tucked up against her chest, and thought about F'han Lha. F'han, whose descendants she had wiped out of history. All to save herself.

The morality of it was too big for her. All she'd been doing was following her training, damn it.

Wake was no hero. She wouldn't pretend to be. She'd been out here doing a job, for a fixed term, for a salary. Now things had gone wrong, and she just wanted to go home. Lying down and dying wasn't in her job description.

That ought to be enough morality for anybody.

It hurt her to think about it.

SHE CLIMBED, WITHOUT regret, back into Pod.

"Instructions."

"Open on request." *From the rescue team, golden, wise advanced.* "Or on reverse of oxygen trend. Or on detection of significant terrestrial biomass. Or–"

She hesitated.

Pod waited, infinitely patient.

"Or, after five million years."

She enfolded the locket in her hand. She was shamed to realise that its tiny failure upset her more than the death of this alien world. She rested her closed fist on her chest.

She closed her eyes.

SHE WAS IMMERSED in white. Pod's canopy was so badly scarred and frosted over she couldn't see out of it.

She lifted her hand from her chest. Dust trickled out of her closed fist. That had been the locket. *Oh, shit.*

"How long?"

Pod's voice was blurred by phasing. "Five million–"

The canopy opened, but with a creak. Thick, ancient ice snapped away from the hinge. Air flooded in, needle-cold.

It was day, again, in this remote future. The sky was still green-blue. She stood. Save for her boots she was naked, her flight suit long rotted away.

The ground was still ice-bound, locked by permafrost. There were layers upon layers of ice now, the ash of burned biomass long buried. The valley—desolate, empty—fell away from her towards a white-flecked sea, apparently unchanged. She felt her lungs drag at the air. She could check with Pod, but she was sure the oxygen content hadn't increased.

Before Pod, there was a neat disk of melted mud, a hundred feet wide, set in the white-coated ground. As she watched, a huge bubble rose and broke, belching, from its interior.

She took a multiprobe from Pod and stepped, stiffly, out of the compartment.

She could feel the cold of the ground through her boots. Her lungs ached already. She couldn't feel her bare skin, but she could see the goosebumps down her arms, see the frosting of her breath. She couldn't stay out here for long.

She reached the melted circle, and thrust in the probe.

There were aminos and nucleotides and sugars in there. There were organisms which had evolved, significantly, from her gut bacteria. *How about that. Maybe the plan is going to pay off.*

Naked, alone in the spacetime pit, shivering over the muddy, primeval pond, she laughed at herself.

IT WAS LATE afternoon, here, five million years deep in the future. She decided to use up another few precious hours of consciousness, to see the night fall. She climbed back into Pod and tried to get warm, wrapping her arms round her bare body.

She plumbed Pod's memory for details of photosynthesis. That was what her little colony needed, to become self-sustaining, to feed from the plentiful sunlight. Pod told her that the first photosynthetic organisms on Earth were colonies of bacteria. They left behind fossils the size of basketballs, called stromatolites…

Wake tried to listen, but could take in very little of this, could make no plans on the basis of the information. She didn't have any resources, anyhow. Her gut-bacteria children would have to make their own way.

Night fell. The stars came out. She inspected the sky. Five million years was enough time to colonise the Galaxy. So close to Earth as this, she'd expect to see *signs*: stars rearranged to suit human needs, encased in immense structures, Dyson spheres.

The constellations she saw were random, the spaces between them empty, unstructured.

Was humanity extinct, then? Or fallen back to Earth, its grandiose ambitions lost?

She was alone here.

She lay back in her couch, and let the sub-dermals crawl over her, unfeeling.

"Instructions."

When you're in a pit, and you can't climb out, what do you do?

You keep digging, she told herself.

"Half a billion years," she said.

RAIN PELTED AGAINST the canopy, thick, heavy drops. Beyond Pod was darkness.

Her boots had gone, and so had most of the soft material in Pod; only hard surfaces remained.

She climbed out. The rain fell against her face. It was warm. When she touched her scalp she found no hair. No eyebrows, lashes, pubic hair.

It looked like day, but the clouds were thick, heavy. She couldn't see anything of the valley, but the basic geology seemed more or less unchanged. On this little plateau the ice was gone, the ground turned uniformly to mud. Her feet sank into the ground; she found it hard to pull her ankles free for each new step.

She couldn't even tell where her primeval-life pond had been.

She let the rain run into her mouth. It was silty, muddy, salty. Sea-bottom mud.

This planet had suffered an impact: a comet, an asteroid maybe.

It happened, in every stellar system, if you hung around long enough. Life on Earth had been obliterated dozens of times, by impacts in the primeval Solar System, before catching hold. Maybe it had happened here.

She dug around in Pod, in the intervals she could function outside the canopy, trying to see if she could recreate her nutrient pond. But most of Pod's systems had failed, or were rotting away. Pod had been smart, she saw, in cannibalising its own components in order to keep the basic life support functions operating. *Good design, by some anonymous engineer a half-billion years dead. Stretching my handful of days across aeons, always diminishing but never finishing, like a paradox of infinite convergent series...* She wasn't expert enough to see what she could take out of this mess and use, that wouldn't finally wreck Pod.

Maybe it didn't matter. If her gut-bacteria babies had survived the impact, maybe they were flourishing, scattered, breeding, somewhere on this warm, wet world. There was nothing more she could do, anyhow.

She brushed the rain off her flesh, as best she could, and climbed back into Pod.

"Instructions."

She listened to the rain against the canopy. It reminded her of L5: the artificial rain storms beating against the walls, when she'd cradled Ben until he'd slept.

She was taking great strides into her pit now, leaping from home in huge logarithmic strides.

"Let's see if the series converges," she said.

"Instructions."

"I'm sorry, Pod. Five billion years."

SHE COULDN'T GET out of Pod.

Out there it was hot enough now to melt lead, so hot she'd be immediately killed. And besides there was no oxygen.

The clouds overhead were thick, unbroken. A diffuse yellow light shone over baked, shattered ground. Even the geology had evolved: the emptied ocean bed was lifted up, the old mountains eroded and dipped.

Now Pod rested on a plain of shattered, broken plates.

Pod had been forced to repair essential subsystems with raw materials taken from the planet. She could see, through the canopy, that it looked as if Pod's base had melted, flowed across square metres of the landscape, seeping into the fabric of this world.

All the oxygen in the air was gone, and carbon dioxide had baked out of the vanished ocean, the rocks, to form a blanket over the planet. The planet had become a Venus; it had fallen into the other classic stable-climate model, for a dead terrestrial world.

Her life seed had failed.

So much for the plan.

Pod showed her images it had gathered, through breaks in the clouds, and from non-optical sensors. The sun had grown huge, and it hovered on the south-western horizon.

This battered old world had become tidally locked to its parent.

And there were fewer stars in the sky, it seemed to her.

She'd come so far, the galaxy itself was starting to die.

She lay down. The sub-dermals were faulty, and she had to lift them into place.

"Instructions."

She felt a morbid curiosity. *I want to see how it finishes.*

"Go on. Indefinitely."

"Instructions."

"Until something changes, damn it."

Maybe something would turn up, as the laws of physics unravelled.

Sure. Her situation was ridiculous. It was still less than a week, subjectively, since she'd taken that sauna in Mother, before descending on this routine survey. Now, she was probably the only human left alive, anywhere.

I wish I'd died, when Shuttle came down. At least those damn Eetees would have enjoyed a little life.

She closed her eyes.

THERE WAS A dull red glow beyond the canopy. She sat up, entrapped like some homunculus in a bell-jar. Through the crystal's protection she could feel the temperature. *Too damn hot.* Pod was failing at last.

It was almost a relief.

The red glow was nothing to do with the Venusian clouds, which had burned away. So had the rest of the atmosphere, in fact. The planet was more like the Moon now: cracked, battered, ancient. Pod had half-melted into the regolith coating the planet, a thin dust gardened by aeons of micrometeorite strikes.

The red glow was the G8-class sun. It was leaving the Main Sequence. Its core, exhausted of hydrogen, had collapsed; helium was fusing now, pumping energy into the outer layers, ballooning them out in a last, extravagant gesture. Soon, all the system's inner planets would be consumed. Including this one.

The warmth was pleasant. It reminded her of the Shelter on L5. When Ben had been small, and still hers.

"Crew loss scenario," said Pod.

"It's all right," she said. "Don't be frightened."

The canopy dissolved, and light enfolded her.

GREEN-EYED MONSTER

THE NIGHT I died, I felt great.

I emerged from the Wheatsheaf at closing time, filled with the euphoria you get from downing a gallon of ale on a balmy mid-summer's night.

I walked down the country lane towards home. The light of the half-full moon cast a cool white glow over the beads of dew on the grass.

I'm a happy drunk, the kind of chap who will express samurai-like loyalty to you over the fourth pint. (Anne, my wife, used to say that I was compensating for being such a sour bastard the rest of the time.) And, sometimes, when the amounts and the ancillary ingredients are just right, the booze will work its mysterious magic on me and make the world seem a fine and wondrous place.

That night was just such an occasion.

I passed the field where I'd been walking with Lizzie, my daughter, earlier that day. We'd found an odd disc-shaped object there, half-buried in the ground. I'd thought of getting on to the local paper about it; maybe they could run a story in their crop-circles column. But then Lizzie had found a toad, a great big ugly brute, which she'd insisted on picking up, cuddling and taking home. The kid has her drunken father's goodness about her, I thought in my maudlin way, and I smiled.

The artefact was still there, I noticed. It was a frisbee maybe a yard across, wedged into the ground so that only half its disc was showing. It glowed softly, with yellow light from some internal source. Odd, of course. But the rational bits of my brain had long since shut down, and I just revelled in the glow, as it beat across the grass to my face.

I thought of Lizzie and the bond she'd formed with the toad. I thought of all the living things around me, the blades of grass and the trees and insects and birds and amphibians and little scurrying mammals, with their tiny lives and consciousnesses glowing like dew drops, all of us bonded by that yellow glow, all united in the great River of Life that flowed from the primeval ocean itself.

Or perhaps towards it. Wrestling with the metaphor, I strolled on.

Anyhow it was a beautiful feeling, a fine moment. Like that Michael Jackson song about the elephant's tusk. My heart was full of joy.

I got home. I didn't want to disturb anybody, so I collapsed on the settee in the living room. I was expecting a bad head in the morning, nothing more.

That much, in retrospect, I might have deserved.

I HAD ONE hell of a dream, that night.

There was gritty red sand under my belly. I was trying to crawl, I realised, my four legs splayed around me, my flippers pawing the dry grains.

I had eight toes on each flipper, webbed over by scaly flesh. And I wasn't so much crawling as slithering, like a snake, my body long and sinuous.

I could barely move. I felt cold, the thin air harsh on my skin.

The land was flat and bare. There was no grass, though there were some plants: mostly small, herb-like growths, and some kind of tumble-weed.

There was no sound save a low, moaning wind. The sky was covered with thick cloud. Actually it reminded me of Cleethorpes.

A few feet away was a pond, a murky, shallow puddle. At its edge was a creature like a newt, lying on its side, already dead.

I seemed to be trying to reach the puddle.

A thing like a centipede scuttled past my nose. I reached out my tongue. In the water, I'd have caught the creature. Here, so high, I could barely move.

This is one hell of a dream, I thought, hangover or not.

I turned, slithering.

I coughed. Brackish water spewed out of my mouth.

I felt as if I was drowning. I sucked at the thin, cold air.

I felt a gill-flap on the back of my head close up. But air scoured in through my nostrils, and into my lungs.

I breathed!

I scrabbled, the air like fire in my new lungs, my belly and tail working at the sand, striving to get to the drying puddle...

I WOKE UP with relief.

Christ, I thought. The mother of all nightmares.

When I opened my eyes and my vision cleared, things seemed a little odd.

I found I was no longer on the settee. I was still in the living room, but viewing it from an angle wholly new to my experience. I was three feet off the floor, in one corner of the room, and seemed to be peering through glass.

Maybe I was still dreaming. Maybe I was stuck inside the TV.

Except...

The glass curved all around me. I was not inside the TV at all. I was in the goldfish bowl, on top of the TV.

I was trying to work this out when I saw the body.

It was sprawled out on the settee, belly up, eyes open and staring at the ceiling. I had never before seen a dead body, and I was shocked.

All the more, because the body was mine.

My body—the body I now inhabited—was a brown sack, covered with warts. My underside seemed to be coated with slime. I had two little arms—with four long fingers each—and two big fat legs, five toes apiece.

Everything seemed dazzling bright, all around me, and I had an unaccountable urge to climb under a rock until nightfall.

I felt an uncomfortable pressure in my rear end. Without thinking about it, I pushed myself up with my little arms, and arranged my legs in an M-shape around my slippery backside.

I felt myself shudder, and a wave of pleasure broke over me.

I seemed to have developed three-hundred-and-sixty-degree vision, and I could see I had deposited a little pellet on the glass behind me.

Holy smoke, I thought.

I was the enormous, ugly toad Lizzie had triumphantly borne into the house yesterday afternoon.

Not only that, but I'd just had a dump in a goldfish bowl.

I just *had* to be dreaming... Didn't I?

At that moment, Lizzie bounded out of bed and started her six-year-old assault on the new day. I heard the thud of her feet on the parquet flooring of her bedroom. She pattered across the landing and stomped down the stairs. I watched as the door to the living room opened and her fuzzy blonde curls appeared. She was wearing her Mickey Mouse pyjamas, with one leg rucked up past the knee. I wanted to take her in my arms and protect her from what she was about to discover.

She walked into the room and stood before the settee, her belly defiantly out-thrust.

After a second or two of blinking contemplation, she reached out a stiff forefinger and poked me—the body—in the ribs.

No response, of course.

"Daddy?"

She climbed onto the settee, then scaled the rounded mound of my stomach. She reached forward and slapped the pale cheek of my corpse with her tiny palm.

The corpse emitted a long, low fart.

Lizzie spilled onto the carpet and ran crying from the room. "Mummy, Mummy!"

By now I had control of my obese, slimy body. I could move its limbs, hop restrictedly around the bowl, blink my bulbous eyes and even croak.

What a mess. I croaked a lonely, plaintive lament, my vocal sac quivering.

Movement in the room beyond the bowl... Anne entered, followed by Lizzie.

"Richard?" she said, moving past the settee and drawing the curtains. "Do you really think this is a good example to set? How many times have I told you that four pints is your limit? Any more and, well... just look at you."

Then, for the first time, she did look at me.

"Richard? Richard..."

Knuckle in her mouth, she advanced tentatively on the settee, reached out and shook my—the body's—shoulder.

"Oh my God…"

What did I expect? A nervous breakdown? Wild hysteria? At least a few tears.

Okay, so we'd had our differences of late…

Business-like, Anne scooped Lizzie onto her hip, crossed the room to the telephone-table next to the TV, and picked up the phone.

While she dialled, I tried to attract her attention. I puffed myself up to twice my size, stretched out all four limbs, and lowered my head to the bottom of the bowl. I'd have scared the crap out of another toad, but Anne didn't even notice me.

"Hello… yes. I need an ambulance. My husband… I think my husband is dead."

There, as bluntly as that. She gave her name and address and replaced the receiver, then hurried from the room.

I subsided like a pricked balloon.

Was this a common thing, I wondered? Did we all, when we died, transmigrate to the bodies of whatever animal was in the vicinity? In other words, were many thousands—nay, millions—of animals now roaming the face of the Earth bearing the souls of deceased human beings?

I had to dismiss the notion as absurd.

But, then, the situation *was* absurd!

I gave up. My metaphysics isn't good at the best of times… Besides, I was starting to feel hungry.

My reverie was interrupted by Anne, entering the room once again. This time she was without Lizzie. She crossed to the phone table, averting her eyes from the corpse.

She dialled quickly. To my experienced eye, she seemed nervous.

"Hello? David, is that you?"

"..."

"Listen to me—he's dead."

"..."

"Who do you think? Richard, my husband. He's lying on the couch stone cold dead. Of course I'm sure. No, no. I'm okay."

"..."

"Oh, well. Yes. Come over. I don't suppose we're going to have to pretend for much longer anyway..." She smiled. "No, we've no need to wait for the weekend, now."

My mind raced.

The weekend? My God... She'd told me she'd be away for two days on business. We knew three Davids, and now I had to guess which of them was conducting an affair with my wife!

As long as it wasn't that egotistical creep, David Munn. Surely it couldn't be...

"..."

"And I love you, too. Bye."

Love! she'd said. *Love*...

I jumped up and down the concave side of the fishbowl like a madman... or, rather, like a mad toad. I croaked in pain and exasperation. I wept real tears of amphibian grief. At least, I think I did. I even lost control of my bladder.

Dying and coming to life in the body of a toad was one thing. But having my wife conducting an affair with some arsehole called David really made me flip.

Oblivious of my antics, Anne hurried from the room.

I wasn't about to sit around and do nothing. I've always been a man of action.

Gathering all my resolve, I squatted, kicked out, and made a spectacular leap from the bowl.

I landed with a wet thud on the Axminster. With no time to lose, I set about arranging Lizzie's building blocks, nudging them into place with my slimy nose.

The ambulance arrived five minutes later. Anne showed two paramedics into the room. I hopped under the television, away from the giant, stomping feet.

One of the paramedics conducted a quick examination. He stood and addressed Anne quietly.

"I'm sorry. It looks like a coronary. Probably instantaneous. You couldn't have done anything."

Anne just nodded, feigning distress.

I willed one of the paramedics to glance down at the lettered blocks I'd arranged across the carpet.

HLEP

Dammit! But I couldn't hop out and rearrange the blocks now, for fear of being trampled.

The paramedics left the room and returned with a stretcher. I hopped up and down next to my desperate message, even croaked at the top of my tiny lungs.

To no avail.

As the medics were unfolding the trolley stretcher, one of them kicked the blocks across the room.

Lizzie ran into the room, stood watching wide-eyed as the paramedics loaded the body onto the stretcher. I hopped over to my daughter and jumped on her foot.

She looked down at me and smiled. Bless her.

I quickly hopped back to my message and croaked.

Lizzie ran over to the blocks. I rolled each one in turn with my nose.

HELP

"Mummy!" Lizzie yelled. "Look, Mummy!"

Abstractedly, Anne turned and read my heart-felt cry. I could have leapt with joy.

Anne nodded. "Very clever, Liz. But not now, okay?"

Exasperated, I watched the medics carry my corpse from the room, followed by Anne and my daughter.

Helpless, I hopped back under the TV, where I felt oddly safe.

Something moved in front of me, small and fast, blurring by.

I didn't even think about it. My long toes twitched, and my tongue snapped out.

My big jaws closed, crushing something. It had a crunchy skeleton and at least six legs: an ant, or a beetle, I guessed.

As I munched at my prize, I was crushed by existential despair.

What a day, I thought.

THERE WAS A manly knock at the door.

A tall, bronzed figure walked into the living room and took my wife in his arms. I could only stare, my toothless mouth agape with rage, jealousy and disbelief.

Christ! Not him. Of all the Davids she could have chosen—not him! David Munn, all cravat, Rayban sunglasses and medallions, was a nasty Afrikaaner thug recently arrived in Britain from Durban.

He was accompanied today, as ever, by Freddy, his pet chimpanzee. He claimed that he'd rescued Freddy from poachers in Zaire. A likely story! Dressed in cut-off jeans and a white t-shirt, the chimp sat at his feet while Munn hugged Anne.

Of all the strange events of the day, this I found the hardest to stomach.

"It must have been a terrible shock," the bastard said. I could almost hear the delight in his voice.

"It was so... so unexpected," Anne replied, wiping an imaginary tear from the corner of her eye. "I mean, God knows, I no longer felt... *love* for Richard. But we had been together for more than ten years. It was such a shock."

Munn there-there'd her with oleaginous platitudes. He even had the gall to offer financial help with the funeral arrangements. Good God—the man was so flagrantly transparent. It was bad enough to know that I was being cuckolded, but to think that Anne had chosen to replace me with this smarmy creep...

It was enough to make my blood boil, even though I was now, technically speaking, a cold-blooded creature.

Suddenly Lizzie knelt down in front of me. Her face lit up with delight. "Mr Toad! I thought you'd gone!"

She lifted me up and held me, legs dangling, before her face. "You know what, Mr Toad?" she whispered. "Daddy went to heaven today. Mummy says he's living with the angels now. You know what as well? Mummy asked me if I'd like David Munn as my new Daddy. I said no way, José!"

My rage at Anne was quelled by a paternal delight with my daughter. I could see that we were going to have a beautiful relationship.

Anne glanced across the room at Lizzie. "Is that that disgusting creature you brought in the other day? Really," she said in an aside to Munn, "I don't know what Richard was thinking about—allowing that repulsive thing in the house."

Munn grinned at my wife. "I wonder if it's the type you can lick and get high?" He eyed me speculatively.

I was rigid with horror. The thought of Munn's tongue on my belly—

Anne snapped, "Don't be disgusting, David."

"I thought you liked me to be disgusting," he said. And he ran his manicured hand over her breast.

I croaked. I pulsed with impotent rage.

Something was happening to my skin. Dark pods were erupting all over me. I felt a powerful urge to clasp something big, soft and cool...

It was the last humiliation. I was getting turned on by what Munn was doing to my wife.

Anne heard my croaking. "Madame, take that toad and put it right back where you found it, this minute."

"But Mummy, it's a clever toad."

"I said this very minute!"

"Oh!" Lizzie flounced to her feet, grabbed me with bad grace, as if I had offended her, and stormed from the house. I hung upside-down, and with my last glimpse of the living room I saw Munn reach out for my wife's hip.

LIZZIE MARCHED DOWN the length of the back garden, singing 'Postman Pat' to herself. We passed through the gate into the meadow, and Lizzie strode towards the oak tree. She stopped and looked about, frowning in concentration. "Now... where was it?"

She started, as if with recollection, and ran around the tree. "Here we are!" She held me out before her with both hands. "Is this your home, Mr Toad?"

I was dangling inches above the curved rim of the disc-like, metal object half-buried in the soil. There was an opening in the rim.

Before I could gather my senses, she dropped me into the hole. Due to the tilt of the object, I slithered down what was obviously the entrance.

I fetched up against a cold surface inside the disc's dim interior. In seconds my eyes adjusted to the reduced light. I stared.

Across the slanting circular floor, watching me, was what I can only describe as... as a *monster*.

Granted, it was a small one—perhaps half the size of my bulbous toad's body—but what it lacked in size it made up for in ugliness.

It was lizard-like, and bipedal, and egg-yolk yellow. Its mouth was wide and filled with a hundred sharp, evil teeth. And its eyes... I will never forget the creature's eyes... its eyes glowed bright green in the dimness of the ship.

We stared at each other. I realised that it must have been as surprised to see me as I was to see it. Tough luck, I thought bitterly. Then it moved.

Lightning-quick, it dashed across to a console set in the wall of the disc. Its stick-thin arm shot out, and a tiny finger depressed a button, and—

I TOOK A halting step forward. The dust seemed to crunch beneath my feet, like a covering of snow. My footprints were miraculously sharp, as if I was walking on fine, damp sand.

The ground was tan brown, the sky utterly black.

I was standing in a broad, shallow crater. Low hills shouldered above the close horizon. There were craters everywhere, ranging from several yards to a thumbnail in width, the low sunlight deepening their shadows.

I was enclosed in some kind of suit; I heard a whirr of pumps and fans, the hiss of rather stale air across my face. There was a pack on my back, so massive I had to tip forward to compensate. But I had little sensation of weight.

I turned. A hundred yards distant there was a spaceship, a glistening, filmy construct of gold leaf and aluminium, bristling with antennae and rocket nozzles.

And here came an astronaut. He looked like a human-shaped beach ball, his suit brilliant white, bouncing over the lunar landscape.

Good grief, I thought. What a dream. Now I'm on the moon.

But at least I'm human again.

I tipped back on my heels and looked up.

The sky was black, empty of stars. But the Earth was a fat crescent, four times the size of a full moon...

I WOKE WITH a start. Actually, I thought I was still half-asleep; my eyes were closed and I had a feeling of falling.

I tried to understand what was happening to me. What was the meaning of these bizarre dreams? And what relationship could they have to this experience of metamorphosis?

There was a pattern, though. In the first dream I had been an amphibian, enduring one of the first forays onto dry land. (How long ago? Three hundred, four hundred million years?) And in the second I was an astronaut, taking the first footsteps on more unexplored territory: the moon. Another evolutionary jump, I supposed.

I felt vaguely excited as I thought it through. After the first dream I'd returned as an amphibian—a modern descendant of that primitive pioneer. That couldn't be a coincidence…

So why, I wondered, hadn't I returned after the second dream as Buzz Aldrin?

It was so unfair.

Only then did I become fully aware of my physical situation. I opened my eyes, alarmed.

I was falling.

There were fluffy clouds below me; I could see a patchwork of ground—small fields, glowing green, typically English—spread out like a tabletop beneath me.

It was rather like being in a plane, coming in to land at Heathrow.

Except I was plummeting, the detail exploding at me.

I seemed to be spinning. I could see a church spire, pointing up like an arrow towards me, a train of black cars outside, their roofs shining like beetles' shells...

I panicked. I started to struggle.

I had new muscles across my chest. They seemed immensely strong. I pulled my arms downwards...

My arms and hands were spindles of bone, trailing sheets of smooth black feathers. Wings. I looked down at my body; it was a compact cone shape, coated with smooth black contour feathers, and my legs were little orange stubs, tucked up beneath me.

I'd been switched again. I was a bird... a crow who didn't know how to fly.

I continued to fall, tumbling, and I opened my mouth—my jaw was heavy and long, extended into a beak—to cry out. A mournful 'caw caw' issued from my throat.

I tried to relax. I was a bird, not a pilot in some feathery aircraft; I should just let this body get on with what it knew best, rather than try to figure out its operation.

I closed my eyes and imagined I was flying, smooth and serene, down towards the church.

When I opened my eyes I *was* flying. Without conscious control, my wings worked at the air in a figure-of-eight motion. As my chest muscles pumped, I could feel the lift of the air flowing over my feathers. My big powerful lungs sucked in oxygen, and my heart rattled, burning up the energy that was maintaining my flight.

It was beautiful, and exhilarating... but also terrifying. I suppose my instincts were too closely conditioned by all those years as a human being; I couldn't get used to there being *nothing* underneath me.

I concentrated on the scenery, not on myself, and my vertigo receded a little.

I opened up my wing feathers and swooped down towards the church. A funeral was in progress, I saw: those big black cars included a hearse. A coffin was being lowered into the ground.

And there was Anne, tastefully dressed in black. It was hard for me to distinguish her from above, but I couldn't mistake my own wife. Beside her was Lizzie, her little gloved hand tucked into her mother's hand... and there was David Munn, his possessive arm around my wife's shoulders.

It was my own funeral!

I cried out, cawing loudly enough for one or two of the mourners to look up, startled.

I couldn't bear it. I beat my wings and sailed up into the sky. I shot through a layer of low cloud and into clear sunlight. I headed straight into the blinding light, pushing at the air. The ground, with all my shattered dreams, receded beneath me, its colours leaching into the mist. I would fly until I could breathe no longer, or until my wings melted, like that Greek chap...

I suppose I must have blacked out.

WHEN I NEXT came to my senses, I discovered that I was—incorporeal; it was as if the jewel of consciousness which had lain behind my eyes had been plucked out and flung into space.

I did not even have heartbeats to count.

It was impossible to measure time, other than by the slow evolution of my emotions.

Driven by curiosity I began to experiment with my awareness. Physically I was composed of a tight knot of perception; now, cautiously, I began to unravel that knot, to allow the focus of my consciousness to slide over space-time.

Soon it was as if I was flying over the arch of the cosmos, over a sprinkling of galaxies, unbound by limits of space or time.

I allowed my consciousness to soften further, to dilute the narrow human perceptions to which I had clung. Soon there was little of the human left in me. Then, at last, I was ready for the final step.

With the equivalent of a smile, I relaxed. My awareness sparkled and subsided.

I was beyond time and space. The causal river of space and time slid by me, vast and turbulent, and my eyes were filled with the grey light which lies behind all phenomena.

And I was never, I decided, ever going to the Wheatsheaf again, no matter what the guest ale.

I WOKE. I WAS lying in a soft bed. A human bed.

I knew immediately that I no longer inhabited the restrictive form of a toad or a bird. I could feel the weight of arms, legs, skull. I yawned and stretched. It felt wonderful to be the owner of skilful fingers and opposable thumbs!

For a moment I lay there, luxuriating in my relief.

I thought about the half-buried disc into which Lizzie had dropped me, and my encounter with the green-eyed monster. Clearly the alien—what else could it have been?—was responsible for my dreams and transfigurations.

Was it investigating step-changes in human evolutionary history: from sea to land, from Earth to space, from—ultimately—man to superman, to immortal? That night, when I had witnessed the disc glowing in the field, the alien had used me as an unwilling subject, through my consciousness investigating the far past and distant future of the human race.

Which wouldn't have been so bad if the whole process hadn't got so fouled up.

First I had been carelessly returned to the body of an amphibious creature, evidently because of its short distance, in evolutionary terms, from that first land pioneer. And then I had been dropped into another part of the great ocean of life, as a bird. But at least, after this latest transfiguration, I had been returned, once more, to a warm human body.

Not that I really I really cared about all this. The alien probe, the destiny of mankind—even my remarkable experiences—were, frankly, of much less interest to me than my personal concerns.

Thus, I pondered, it has always been.

Even now, I had other things on my mind.

Munn! You bastard!

I opened my eyes.

I RAISED AN arm and stared at it. The arm was long and covered in black, shiny hair. I gazed down at my new body.

My penis was the size of a walnut.

Munn groaned and rolled over. He blinked up at me, grimacing in the morning sunlight. "Freddy, will you please lie down and go to sleep?"

I was the pet chimp of the man who was cuckolding me. And I was sharing the bed with Munn and my wife! It was the final insult.

I leapt out of bed, screeching. This startled Munn, I noted with pleasure. I decided that enough was enough. I was done with these transfigurations, these random jumps around the animal kingdom. Now I was an extra from *Planet of the Apes*. Who could know what I might become next?

I tried to run from the room. I tumbled over, until I worked out how to move on all fours, with my weight resting on my big weightlifter's arms. When I had the hang of it, I ran downstairs.

From the kitchen I collected a box of matches, and from the garage a can of petrol. I loped around the house and through the back garden. It was still early—fortunately there was no one about. I would have presented a strange sight indeed, a secretive chimp scuttling across the field with a petrol can clutched to its chest.

I reached the buried disc. The corpse of a toad, discarded, lay beside it.

I sat on my haunches, unscrewed the lid and tipped the can. The petrol throbbed from the rusting nozzle with agonising slowness. I decided that, all things considered, half a can should do the trick.

I dribbled a trail of petrol across the ground, retreated a few steps, struck a match and threw it.

An instant *whumph!* and the disc snorted a great gout of flame like some enraged, half-buried dragon. A secondary explosion shook the oak, but by this time I was scampering back across the field and into the garden.

I saw Lizzie emerge from the house and stare at the plume of smoke that hung above the field. She had a box of Sugar Puffs clutched under her arm. "What was that, Freddy?" she asked sleepily, rubbing tired eyes.

I paused and regarded her, contemplating our future together.

I might have the body of a chimp, I told myself, but it could have been far, far worse...

I wrapped my head in my arms, which made her laugh, then took her hand and went inside for breakfast.

Now, I thought, for Munn. Now I had strong arms and legs, and teeth as big as the dominoes at the Wheatsheaf. Now we'd see who was the dominant male around here.

Munn, you bastard! I'm coming to get you!

Stephen Baxter and Eric Brown

SUNFLY

ONARA SLIPPED FROM the shuttered darkness of the dormitory when she judged that her fellow apprentice Scholars were asleep. She emerged into bright daylight. The sun—as always—was directly overhead, a kernel of yellow light in the sky's blue bowl.

She was aware of her heartbeat, its frantic drumming accompanying the small voice in her head that told her that what she was doing was forbidden. She crept down the west wing of the Scholars' manse, along the path that passed her teachers' common room. She ducked and hurried beneath the flung-open shutters. A few teachers had still not retired, and she heard the deep voice of Sch. Malken, her own tutor.

She paused on the border of the garden, hidden now by a stand of sweetcorn. Before her, the land to the south rose in a broad sweep of greensward. As she left the cover of the corn and ran up the hillside towards the forest, she knew that all it would take was for one Scholar to glance through the shutters and she would be seen. The consequences of being caught spurred her on: solitary confinement for a week, or, worse, the whip. She dashed into the custody of the forest and collapsed behind the bole of a tree, breathing hard.

She gazed back down the hillside, following the curve of the land to the north. From her place of shade, she could see the Vale with the sprawling timber edifice of the manse cupped in its palm, and the patchwork design of the crop fields surrounding it. The sunlight beat down, flattening the panorama; the only shadows were tiny pools of darkness beneath the larger trees.

As she followed the lie of the land further to the north, she saw how the fields and copses at the far side of the Vale merged into a fine band of blue and green, and were finally lost in the mist at infinity. And beyond the horizon, the land leapt upwards to become a great wall plastered with sun-glistening lakes and rivers, a wall which reached into the sky, narrowing as it rose.

She lifted her head back and squinted to shut out the sunlight. She could just make out a fine, perfect line crossing the sky and piercing the disc of the unmoving sun. The World was a hoop, suspended around the sun, and that line across the heavens, bluer than the blue of the sky, was a strip of landscape beyond the sun—a land perhaps peopled by humans as was her own Vale, or perhaps inhabited by monsters, like the Foe which had haunted her childhood nightmares.

But now a shadow fell on her face, and she felt the air grow chill. Clouds crossed the sun, and a flock of birds—

high and tiny—fled with them to the south. Such migrations were a new feature in her World; nobody knew what they meant—or rather, nobody would tell her.

Again she studied the arch of the landscape which rose beyond the northern horizon. She scanned down the column of land, until she found the point where it almost thinned to invisibility. The Narrowing, as she had heard the Scholars call it, had appeared two months ago, causing much comment and speculation among the apprentice Scholars.

It looked as if the World-band had been stretched almost to breaking point. She shivered. The Narrowing was deeply disturbing to her, a fault in the structure of the World.

RESTED, SHE STOOD and ran easily through the shadowed forest, no urgency in her progress now, just anticipation.

She came to the glade, a moss-lined bowl shaded by the foliage high above. Rarely was she here before Kallis—he had the freedom of the forest, whereas she had to wait until the time was right to leave her dorm. Alone, now, she felt vulnerable. What if she fell prey to the wild hornbeasts which stalked the forest? Or even—she shivered—one of the Foe?

She chastised herself for being so childish. Hadn't Kallis told her that even wild hornbeasts were wary of man? And as for the Foe—what were they but the creatures of legend? She fingered the leather choker about her neck, a present from the hunter on their very first tryst.

She jumped at a touch to the back of her neck. "Kallis! You fool!" She hugged him as he laughed at her fright.

He pulled away and regarded her, his eyes bright blue in his sun-weathered face. There was something remote about his expression, she saw through her pleasure. "Come," he said. "Last time I saw you we talked about strange happenings. The clouds, the northerly winds... Now I want to show you something even stranger."

Without a further word he took her hand and pulled her through the forest, heading east.

They ran swiftly through the undergrowth, Kallis's cross-bow creaking against his leathers, his footsteps hunter-fleet. She felt her hand enclosed in his strong yet gentle grip, like a small bird.

They must have run for miles. Soon Onara judged that they were approaching the eastern extremity of the forest. Despite Kallis's reassuring smile, she detected unease in his manner. She wondered if he wished to talk about his declaration, three sleeps ago, that he and a group of fellow Hunters were planning to leave the area. She hoped he'd abandoned the idea; she couldn't imagine how she might live without her lover, even for a short time.

The forest thinned; great, old trees gave way to shrubs and bushes. Kallis draped an arm around her shoulder and walked her to the edge of the forest. They climbed a high escarpment and looked down across a valley that widened to a broad plain.

She glanced northwards, into the sky. The clouds had cleared, and the Narrowing seemed more sharply defined than before. Was it closer? Was the Narrowing passing along the length of the World-wheel, towards her?

Kallis pointed to a place on a hillside, far to the east. "Look. See there!"

She saw what she thought at first was the dark shadow of a cloud, rushing over the sunlit landscape. Then the shadow changed shape—too rapidly for a cloud—and transformed itself from a long ellipse into an oblate blob. Now it changed direction, flowing down a valley like a viscous fluid.

"What is it?"

"Hornbeast, Onara. A massive herd of hornbeast." Now she saw real concern etched into his sun-beaten features. "It is as I have told you. They're leaving their stamping grounds. And not only hornbeast. Other animals too. Everything we hunt. Everything we depend upon to survive. They're all leaving." Kallis looked down at her, his expression troubled. "Winter," he said, experimenting with the unfamiliar word. "You told me that Winter was approaching—that Winter is at the heart of this. Have you found out what a Winter is?"

She avoided his gaze. "I'm sorry. I've tried. Scholar Malken won't answer. He knows something—I know he knows—but he's keeping the knowledge to himself."

Over the years, she was coming to realise, the Scholars had taught her little but the basics of reading and writing. Oh, she had studied the geometry of the World, and had read the epic poems of times past, the plays about the daily life of the ancients—but even in this literature there was a singular lack of genuine enquiry. The origin of humankind's past, she felt, was a closed book—and she was coming to understand that the future was similarly closed. Even about something as fundamental, and dangerous, as this mysterious Winter, she'd been able to piece together no more than fragments of lore.

"Winter is... I think it's a period of shadow, of cold. Of darkness." She paused. "I understood too that it is dangerous, this Winter."

Kallis snorted. "Dangerous? How can shadow be dangerous? And darkness. I know darkness only when I close my eyes or secure the shutters on my hut. And what is cold? I know what heat is. But how can I imagine cold?" He shook his head. "Life without heat?"

"Kallis, other things have been happening in the manse. Strange things. Three of my friends have disappeared over the past six sleeps. One lesson they were there, and then they were gone. No explanation. Almora... my closest friend. Just gone."

He glanced at her. "It might have something to do with..." he gestured at the clouds, the fleeing hornbeasts— "with this?"

"I don't know—but maybe. All these strange things at once—maybe they're connected. Also, Scholars have disappeared. They seem ill, slow and feeble, and then they go." She tried to remember if Almora had seemed sickly. She had noticed nothing very amiss; perhaps her friend had been quiet, withdrawn. Or perhaps she was being wise after the event.

Kallis said, "The Scholars do know something. I'm convinced of that. We were riding north of here through Jade Valley, two sleeps ago. We saw a plantation, heavily guarded by Scholars. The plants were like nothing I've seen before—tall, blood-red flowers. We were told to move on. The guards were armed with cross-bows."

They stood and stared down into the valley.

She wanted to ask him if he had yet made his decision to leave with the Hunters, but the words stuck in her throat. Kallis moved a hand to the small of her back, rubbing the base of her spine in the way he knew she liked. She tried to forget what might lie ahead, and reached up for his lips.

He found a grassy bank where they made love, Kallis as careful and gentle as ever, as if she were a fragile object that might break with rough handling. Even at the height of his passion he was restrained—his gentleness seemingly emphasized by his bulk. For a while her worries were banished, only for them to return tenfold as they lay side by side and stared up at the sunlight streaming down through the tree-tops.

From a branch above her head dangled a cluster of sunfly pods. The pods were only partly formed—small, open balls of webbing, suffused with sunlight—and inside them larvae could be seen, patiently building. Idly she watched the tiny motion, lost in the detail of it. One larva was proceeding more slowly than the rest; its pod was barely half completed. She pointed this out to Kallis.

He smiled. "That one doesn't want to be a sunfly," he said. "Perhaps he likes being a larva."

"Or perhaps it's the change he's scared of. Nobody likes change, I suppose."

The silence stretched, and she knew what he was thinking.

"Kallis..."

"Mmmm?"

"What you said before, about leaving...?"

He sighed. "The Hunters must go. Our prey have fled south, and so we're going after them, into the mountains." He mussed her hair. "We are Hunters. We can't live on sweetcorn alone, Onara."

"But how can you outrun Winter?"

He frowned. "I don't know. But what else can we do? Where else could we run? The Edges?"

"The Edges?" she repeated, startled. The Edges were invisible mountains—it was said—at the east and west borders of the World, bad-lands inhabited by strange beasts, madmen and the Foe. She had heard many horror stories of the Edges, most no doubt apocryphal, designed to scare children, warn off adventurous adolescents from ever straying. But if only a tenth of the tales were true…

"They say no one ever returns from the Edges."

Drily, he said, "You're supposed to be a Scholar's apprentice. Do you know anyone who's actually been there, Onara?" When she failed to reply, he went on, "There are other tales. The Hunters have legends, stories, about warriors who trek for days through the bad-lands, who discover wondrous lands beyond, and bountiful hunting grounds. Who knows what the truth is?"

He took her hand. "Come with me, Onara. Leave behind your studies. You said yourself you have grown to hate the manse."

"You won't be coming back?"

"Who knows what we'll be doing? If this Winter is as dangerous as you make out… Onara, I want you with me."

"I don't know! I need time to think. So many strange things are happening. For so long my life has been ordered, regulated. And now everything is changed."

"I'll be leaving at the first hour two sleeps from now," Kallis said in a voice heavy with ultimatum. "I'll meet you in the glade."

IT WAS THE hour before the breakfast call. Onara lay on her pallet in the shuttered darkness, unable to sleep. She would be tired during lessons, and this would be remarked upon by the Scholars, but she no longer feared reprimand.

Events had carried her past the point where she regarded the rules and petty laws of the manse as sacrosanct. Great changes were imminent, whether she left with Kallis or not. She touched the choker at her neck and considered the future.

The next time I rise, she thought, I must decide whether to leave with Kallis.

She settled early to her work. She sat alone in a long cloister, working through a volume of gaudy legends. She was soon bored; she'd studied this material several times before, and was now supposed to commit it to memory. Like so many lessons of late, she thought. I'm learning nothing.

A breath of hot wind blew through the cloister and riffled the leaves of the tome on her desk–

"Onara!"

She jumped.

Sch. Malken was beside the desk, smiling down at her. "My brightest pupil, Onara—a talent wasted in this age." He seemed to be talking to himself; he appeared impatient, disturbed. Sch. Malken was tall, with a full head of dark hair brushed back from a high forehead. He wore the traditional white robes of the Scholar. Many girls envied Onara her tutor, and could not understand her indifference to him.

Now his eyes were on her, deep, searching—they held a hunger she had come to recognise, though it disturbed her.

"Enough of these books. Come with me, Onara. I've something new to show you. The truth."

It was as if he'd been reading her thoughts. She stared at him, astonished.

SCH. MALKEN ESCORTED her to the stables, where he selected a hornbeast. At his gesture, she climbed aboard the broad saddle behind him. They left the manse and moved slowly into the hills which bordered the Vale to the west, and then through a narrow pass and beyond, into a region Onara had never visited before.

The land here was flat and parched, devoid of water and life. She had the impression of great antiquity; the sunlight was like a solid thing, embedding her in this ancient, dead landscape. Yellow dust rose up in great clouds around the hooves of the patient hornbeast, so that Onara was forced to wrap a scarf across her mouth. Her head was filled with the stink of the weary, aged 'beast as it toiled through the pitiless light.

"Where are we going, Scholar Malken?"

He raised his hand in a gesture advising silence and patience.

They followed a path into a widening valley, and at the far end Onara made out a squat, stone-built structure. As they approached, she saw that young Scholars armed with bows guarded the building.

Sch. Malken climbed from the 'beast and helped Onara down. She paused before the building. It had appeared small from a distance, but now it loomed over her, dark and imposing, like the structures she had seen in drawings and paintings in old history books.

The Scholar took her hand and, under the gaze of the guard, escorted her into a shadowy vestibule. Torchlight illuminated a flight of narrow stone steps, descending below ground level. They walked carefully down the steps and stood before a blank stone wall.

Then, as if driven by magic, a section of the wall swung open, and a bright light emanated from the room, illuminating its contents.

Onara could only stare.

A table and two chairs, formed of a white, stone-like material as if extruded from the floor itself, occupied the centre of the room. Sch. Malken gestured Onara inside. Her sandalled feet slapped on the cool surface of the white stone.

On the table stood two goblets.

"What is this place?" she asked.

"It was built by our distant ancestors. We do not know its original purpose." Sch. Malken gestured towards the goblets. "Please, join me. Drink the wine."

He lifted a goblet, smiled at her and drank. With both hands—the goblet was large and heavy—Onara lifted the blood-red liquid to her lips and sipped. It was sweet and as thick as syrup.

As the liquid reached her belly, she felt a bubble of coldness swell out through her system. It was a hard, unpleasant feeling—as if she had been invaded. She put the goblet down and stared at the dregs of the drink.

"What is it?"

"Poppy wine. That's all." He smiled at her. "Onara, I have watched you grow wise enough to understand that there are mysteries beyond your studies. Now, you are ready to learn more. You must have many questions."

At last, she though. But she wondered why he had invited her here—why now, suddenly, he was prepared to be open with her. What did he want with her?

"What is the Narrowing?" she blurted. "And Winter? One day I overheard two Scholars discussing Winter…"

"Understand that although we hold ancient wisdom, Onara, some of the mysteries of our World are beyond even our understanding. We know that every thirty generations a Winter consumes the land—"

"Then Winter is real?"

"Oh, yes, my dear. It is a period without sunlight for thirty generations, a time so cold that nothing will survive on the land. The Narrowing presages this Winter, and the Scholars make preparations—"

"The Scholars come down here," Onara interrupted. "Here, our people can survive the Winter?"

Her tutor inclined his head. "Just so. Now come, this way." He gestured towards a white wall, and as he approached a door-shaped section of it swung open.

Onara followed her tutor into the second, much larger chamber. This one was empty, but for a painting which almost covered one wall.

Onara quailed.

"Go ahead," Malken said. "Study it. It's only an image. It can't hurt you."

Onara approached the image—and discovered that it was not a painting at all. The detail was too fine, too realistic. It was as if a scene from life had been frozen, chiselled into a block, and set into the wall. She could not detect how it had been manufactured.

The picture showed a single, immense beast. Bipedal, it had thick legs and powerful, longer-than-normal arms; and its chest and head were grossly swollen. Its face was a mask of hard blue chitin, and it leered down at Onara with black eyes. It was almost human—a travesty of the human form, but close enough for its horror to be all the greater.

She recognised the beast from a thousand legends. This was the Foe: as terrible as any childhood nightmare, but made real by this extraordinary depiction.

She heard Sch. Malken's voice, rational, reassuring. "Our World is a fortress," he said. "A fortress of light. And beyond the fortress roam beasts like this. The Foe."

"But what is this monster? Where does it come from? How–"

He placed a finger on her lips, silencing her. "In the remote past, we fought such demons. We won—or survived, at any rate—but at a terrible cost.

"Once, Onara, we inhabited the full length of the World. Now we exist in scattered groups of Scholars, Farmers and Hunters. For generations the World sustains us, in reasonable comfort—but then, to survive the Winters, we must resort to—ah—extreme measures."

He moved towards the far wall, and passed through another miraculous doorway. Onara followed. They stood on the threshold of the largest chamber yet, a long, low room receding in perspective. White cots the shape of sunfly-larva pods lined the walls on either side.

Onara stood in the entrance, reluctant to step forward. Ahead of her, Sch. Malken turned and held out a hand. "Come, there is no need to be afraid."

She took his hand and joined him by the first pod. Her stomach turned. The body in the pod was stiffened and bloated, its skin a sickly shade of blue. Its transformation, however, did not prevent her recognition.

"Scholar Greer!" Greer had been Almora's personal tutor...

Sch. Malken drew her towards the next pod. Onara had to force herself to follow him, for she knew what she would find.

Sure enough, Almora lay in the pod, as blue and bloated as her tutor. She was curled up—almost like a child, Onara thought; and yet Almora's limbs were twisted, her blue face distorted, her mouth stretched wide as if in a frozen scream.

"Is she dead?"

Sch. Malken shook his head. "Merely... sleeping. This is encystment, not death. After Winter, when the sunlight returns, Almora and the others will wake and rebuild society."

Onara stared down the length of the chamber. She quickly calculated that approximately a thousand pods occupied the walls.

A thousand? The Farmers, the Hunters—why, there must be ten times as many people in the Vale! "But what of all the others?"

He stood before her, tall, authoritative, his voice gentle. "I am afraid that many will perish as the temperatures drop and ice covers the Vale."

She stared at him. "Some will be left to die?" she asked, incredulous.

"That is the way it has always been."

"But that's..." She was shaking her head at the enormity of what he had said. "That's barbaric." She tried to order her thoughts, marshal pertinent questions. She was aware of his eyes on her, ambiguous, calculating.

"Why was the World built like this, so every Winter so many would perish?"

He stared down at her. "The World was not built by humans," he told her. "And so it was not built for humans. Aeons ago, humans came from other suns in great ships. We found this artifact, this World, deserted. Its builders had long since left, for reasons we do not know. We made the World our home. We battled with the Foe. Over the generations, we lost the ability to travel beyond the World—maybe during the war." He lay a hand on Onara's shoulder. "Long ago, to combat Winter, we developed the means to harvest and prepare the wine of the poppy. Once sealed within this tomb, we will sleep through the Winter like generations of Scholars before us. And when the sunlight returns…"

She stared at him. "We…?" Onara felt the blood drain from her face. I have already drunk the wine, she thought. Already…

"I must become like her, like Almora?"

"As Scholars, our pods are reserved. It will be a new World, Onara." His hand was heavy on her shoulder. "You and I—together in a cleansed, new World."

A FIERCE WIND battered the shutters of the dormitory.

Onara could not sleep. She lay on her pallet and considered all that had happened to her, the choice she had to make. Sch. Malken had promised her salvation from the certain death that awaited if she remained in the Vale, but the images of Almora and Greer returned to her, blue and bloated, and all she could feel was horror.

Onara thought about Kallis and the others left to die— but perhaps Sch. Malken was wrong. Perhaps there was some way to survive on the surface?

Besides—she discovered with wonder, when she looked into her heart—she would rather die with her lover than live the rest of her life with Sch. Malken.

When all the apprentices were asleep, Onara slipped from the dormitory for the last time.

SHE REACHED THE glade in the forest. The dell did not seem the welcoming place she had come to know; the light from above was harsh, the tree-tops stirred by the wind. Kallis was waiting for her, arms folded. His face was set, his eyes troubled; she thought she saw love in his expression, and certainly tenderness, but also a determination that frightened her.

"Well?" His voice was hard. "Have you decided?"

"We have to flee, Kallis."

"I know. I told you—the southern mountains. I have a hornbeast, waiting. We can be there in—"

"No!" The strength in her own voice surprised her. "You don't understand." She told him, rapidly, of what she had learned from Sch. Malken—of the tomb in the desert, the poppy wine.

"You can't outrun the Narrowing, Kallis." She took his hands and pulled him to her. "You must face this. If you follow the herds, you'll be killed, you and all your people—long before you reach the mountains. Even there, you'd find no shelter."

"So we'll die. All of us, except the Scholars. And those they choose to save. No wonder they guard the poppies so well! But why must it be so?" His dropped her hands and fingered his bow, and anger made his eyes hard. "Why not grow more poppies, enough for everyone? No, of course not—they wish to choose who will live with them in the New World. They wish to keep the power to themselves."

The taste of the wine she had already taken, in her ignorance, seemed to burn in her mouth. It was as if she could feel it, heavy in her stomach; she felt shamed, as if she had betrayed Kallis. "None of this matters now, Kallis, I don't care about the Scholars and their poppy wine."

Now, with visible effort, he restrained his anger. "You must care, Onara. Listen to me. Go back–"

"No!"

"You must. If this shelter and the blood of the poppy will save you, then you must return."

She thought of Malken's possessive gaze on her. "I'd rather die with you than go back!" She stepped away from him. "And don't try to force me, Kallis!"

He hesitated, studying her; then he smiled. "I know you too well to try," he said.

She became aware—quite abruptly—of a shift in the light, of shadows which raced across his face. Above them, the wind surged through the foliage.

A branch cracked and fell, not two paces away. She clung to Kallis.

"Is this the end?" he asked. "The end of the World?"

"Maybe the beginning of the end," she whispered. "Come!"

They hurried through the forest, away from the manse. The ground itself seemed to be shuddering now; it groaned in great bass tones like some wounded hornbeast. She had a sudden sense of the fragility of things: the World was, after all, no more than a hoop of soil and air, circling its sun as her choker encircled her throat.

Her gaze was drawn to the darkening sky. Clouds raced across the face of the sun. She looked to the north, followed the neck of the land as it towered over the horizon—

She gasped. The Narrowing had gone. The World-wheel soared up above the air, smooth and unbroken, its remote oceans glittering in the light of the sun.

"What is it?" Kallis asked.

"The far lands, upraised in the sky. Don't you see? The Narrowing has vanished!"

He gazed at her, his mouth open.

"Or perhaps," she said as if to herself, "the Narrowing has merely passed down, out of our sight, into the mists at the horizon. It has journeyed around the sun, and now it has travelled from sky to earth, a great beast tunnelling through the ground towards us…"

"We have to get away," Kallis said. He had to shout above the roaring of the wind. "And there's only one place to go. We have to try for the Edge, Onara."

Numbly, she followed him.

AT THE BORDER of the forest Kallis's hornbeast was waiting, tethered to a tree. It eyed them eagerly, evidently unperturbed by the continued earth-tremors. Bags of victuals were slung over its haunches. When Kallis gave it its head, the 'beast carried them briskly off to the east: towards the nearer Edge of the World. The hornbeast was a young, healthy animal, used to vigorous activity—quite different from the tired old animals kept by the Scholars—and it covered the ground rapidly.

When they reached the crest of the hill that bordered the Vale, Kallis reined in the 'beast. Onara surveyed the little valley where she'd grown up.

She felt a shiver of strangeness—but it was too late now to turn back: she could only imagine how Scholar Malken would punish her for deserting him. And besides, she saw, her home had already changed irrevocably. The continuing tremors and winds were battering at the fences and the fragile timber buildings. Here and there, the people of the outlying farms were struggling to repair the damage, to help the injured; but for the most part the farmers seemed content to wander through the devastation, peering up at a sky which had so rapidly betrayed them.

Kallis touched her hand. "We cannot help them now. Perhaps we can't help ourselves."

She felt anger burn inside her. "They're waiting to die. At least your people are trying, striving to flee."

"Only because Hunters have always travelled… Look." He pointed to the manse at the heart of the Vale. Onara made out a knot of activity there, white-robed Scholars hurrying from the buildings, heading in the direction of the stone tomb in the desert.

"The Scholars have left it late to seek their shelter," Kallis murmured.

"They disgust me," she said. She turned her back on the Vale, and Kallis spurred the 'beast once more.

THE JOURNEY LASTED countless hours.

The hornbeast seemed tireless. More than once its endless motion lulled Onara into a foul, uncomfortable sleep—a doze in which demons of earth and wind howled about her—from which she would awaken to find her arms still wrapped around Kallis's broad chest, the hair of the plodding hornbeast's back coarse under her thighs.

They rode beyond the Vale: they'd gone so far, Onara calculated dully, that they might have passed through ten or twelve Vales laid end to end. The landscape was unchanging—a familiar patchwork of lakes, low hills and woods—though the terrain was wilder here than she was used to.

The disturbances continued. The clouds still fled across the sky, and the land rattled like a drum-skin. Once they had to take refuge in a copse while a great herd of hornbeast swept across the land before them in a tornado of dust, stinking fur and clattering hooves. Their own animal twitched and stirred under them, longing to join its fellows; but Kallis covered its complex triple nostrils with the palm of his hand and murmured to it, soothing.

They encountered no people, though sometimes they passed through rectangular outlines etched in the land, which might once have bordered fields; and in many places they passed the tumbled ruins of what might have been great stone buildings, in the style of the Scholars' shelter. "Another legend verified," Onara told Kallis. "Once, the World far beyond the Vale really was full of people. Perhaps, once, there were humans all the way around the World-wheel—a huge band of people, surrounding the sun."

How ironic it was to learn so much, if she were to die so soon!

Gradually the endless riding wore her down, and she found her thoughts softening, guttering. The landscape changed: it became bare, free of buildings and vegetation. In some places, raw rock showed through the thin covering of soil and dust, like the exposed bones of the World. Onara's chest began to hurt. She panted, dragging at the air, as if it had grown thin and lacking in nourishment. At first she thought that this might be some illness afflicting her alone, but it soon became evident that Kallis, too, was having difficulties. Even the hornbeast growled its breaths, its huge nostrils steaming.

At last there was no past or future for her: only this endless present, the hornbeast beneath her, the broad, anonymous back of the man before her.

SHE WOKE FROM a troubled doze to find that the terrain around them had changed perceptibly. The 'beast's hooves clattered against hard ground. There was no grass here, nor even earth: only a dull substance that returned no light, like hardened wood.

Onara turned and surveyed the way they had come.

It felt as if they were climbing a slope; the ground tilted upwards beneath them—but she knew that there were no mountains here. Looking back, she could see for tens of miles; the land was a plane punctuated by snaking rivers, lakes, splashes of woodland green; hillocks poked through the surface, making the land look as if it had been moulded. All this still looked normal, she thought: solid, inhabitable, eternal, all pinned under the vertical light of the sun. But the whole World had tipped up behind her, like a damaged table: all of it, trees and hillocks and rivers, sloped away impossibly. It was as if she was near the crest of a slope a hundred miles high.

And when she looked ahead, the horizon seemed close, a definite line bathed in a deep blue light.

Kallis reined in the 'beast, then turned to her. "I don't understand." He seemed frightened. "How can the World be tilted like this? Will we fall?"

She studied him. Dust and sweat clung to his face, emphasising the lines of worry there. "I don't think the World has tipped up," she said. Her voice was thick, her thinking cloudy. She struggled to recall what she'd learned in the manse of the geometry of the World. "The floor of the World draws us to it, holds us there. If not–" she waved her hands vaguely—"we'd float off into the air. And now that we're approaching the Edge, I suppose, most of the bulk of the World lies behind us. It's drawing us back. So it seems tipped up to us; it wants us to fall back to its centre." She stared at him, her vision blurring slightly. "Do you see? This feels like a mountain, but it isn't one..." Perhaps, she thought, this is the origin of the legends of the invisible mountains that were the walls of the World.

His returning gaze was uncomprehending, fearful, yet still tender.

She felt a thrumming in the ground beneath them. The 'beast stirred, frightened. The vibration was powerful, even violent; it battered at her bones. Above her, rags of cloud raced across the sun, turbulent and boiling. There was a sense of instability, of huge, imminent change.

"Look," Kallis said, pointing.

In the north, the details of the landscape blurred as ever into the distance, the hillocks and valleys and woods merging into a blue mistiness—but now the land to the north was turning onto its side, the hills, lakes and forests clinging precariously to the slope.

The land was twisting, she saw: all of it, with its freight of trees and seas, as if it were no more substantial than a piece of ribbon.

Horror pushed through her fatigue, the pain in her chest. At last she understood.

Kallis swore. "What demonic vision is this?"

Black spots danced at the borders of her vision; it was hard to think, and she felt an unreasonable irritation at Kallis, at his obtuseness. "It's the Narrowing approaching us. Don't you understand? The Narrowing is not—as we thought—a stretching, a neck in the World; it's a monstrous twisting."

"Then we're dead," he said, his voice thin. "How can we survive such a thing?"

"I don't know," she said. "But we must try. We've come this far. Don't give up, like the others."

Through his mask of dust and fear, he smiled at her, and she saw again the boy she had loved in the woods. He eyed the slope—the apparent slope—before them. "Up there." He pointed. There was a notch in the smooth floor. "Do you think it's a pass through these mountains?"

"There are no mountains," she wheezed, trying to find the words to explain. "And so there is no pass. It's all a matter of geometry–"

"Geometry or not, we'll try for it," he said. With a brisk slap he goaded the hornbeast into fresh motion.

The animal stumbled on the hard surface, and Onara was almost thrown off. She clung to Kallis's back, gasping.

As they climbed, the land beneath the 'beast's hooves tipped up—or seemed to—even further. The air became progressively thinner, the sky a richer blue.

The great Narrowing—or twisting—rushed towards them. The landscape swept up like some beautiful, surreal sculpture, finely detailed; she could even see the thin layer of grey-blue air which enveloped the land, lifted up with it. The substance of the World was obviously flexible enough to permit this twisting about—but she could see how much less resilient was the World's fragile cargo of life. She saw rivers and seas spill from their banks, flooding the land; forests shivered to matchwood, or burst into flame in brief, remote flashes.

Despite the peril of their situation—despite its apparent hopelessness—she felt a vague excitement infuse her as her understanding developed. Our World, she thought, is a hoop—every child knows that—but it is a twisted hoop. And the twist migrates around the land, wreaking its devastation once every so many hundred thousand sleeps...

She considered what Sch. Malken had told her about the origins of the World. Perhaps the twist is a flaw in the World. Was this the reason the original builders fled—because of this... this accidental twisting?

Finally the hornbeast, which had been growing steadily more agitated, would go no further despite all Kallis's gasped blandishments and caresses. Kallis and Onara dismounted and the 'beast clattered back down the slope.

Breathless, already exhausted, Onara and Kallis stumbled onwards. The surface here was hard, almost slippery. Onara kicked off her sandals, and the purchase of her bare feet made the ascent a little easier. But the climb was very steep now, the land behind them tipped up impossibly. The air was so thin it seemed to scratch at her throat as she dragged down painful breaths.

"I feel as if I might let go, and fall forever," Kallis gasped.

"Don't talk," she said. "Just climb…"

But now she could, she realised with vague interest, no longer feel her legs. She toppled forward, and slithered a few paces down the slope before she managed to drag herself to a halt. She lay there, panting.

Kallis scrambled down to join her. He seemed to be tottering, and when he sat beside her it was with a liquid fall, as if he would never rise again.

"No," she gasped. She reached out and grabbed his shoulders, trying to keep him upright. At first his weight bore her downwards, and her arms felt like young twigs, devoid of strength.

Then she felt a bubble of coldness swell out and through her system. It was a hard, unpleasant feeling, and yet brought in its wake a sensation of new strength suffusing her arms and legs. She pushed easily at Kallis and lifted him upright.

She looked at her hands, where they pressed against Kallis's chest. Her knuckles and wrists were swollen, the joints like ripe berries. And a blue, hard sheen lay in patches over her skin. Even as she watched, the blue stain spread further.

The poppy wine, she thought. Is that what's helping me now?

She remembered Greer, and Almora, in the shelter. Now it was happening to her: encystment. She felt an instant of panic. She wasn't in the shelter. Perhaps it wasn't safe to be outside, when the encystment began...

Glancing down in wonder, she saw that her legs had become shorter—thicker—and her chest and belly strained against the fabric of her dress. She was distorting, the blue hardness spreading across her skin like a grotesque infection. She was glad that Kallis was unconscious, that he could not see her like this.

But she had never felt so... so alive, she realised. Her flesh tingled, as if she were growing, changing. Metamorphosing...

So the encystment could kill her, could it? She suppressed an urge to laugh. She could only die once! And if the effects of this encystment enabled her to save Kallis—or at least have a damned good try—then she'd welcome it.

The land, the whole Edge 'slope', shuddered like a living thing. Kallis, unconscious, slumped against her. She glanced up. The twist was so close now that she could see how it progressed, heartbeat by heartbeat, with more landscape being drawn up into it and deformed.

She bent and lifted Kallis. Her new, bulging arms were clumsy, and Kallis moaned as his head rattled against her chest, but when she cradled him he felt as light as a doll.

She began to stride up the 'slope'. Her legs worked steadily, carrying the extra weight. The pass, the notch in the land, seemed closer now, easily accessible. She was becoming something inhuman, but she felt exhilarated. Why, I'm not even out of breath any more–

In fact, she realised, she wasn't even breathing.

She halted, astonished. She stood on the ridge, close to the top of the World, with Kallis's body limp in her arms. She listened to herself: her body was utterly silent, the complex plumbing of her lungs and windpipe and throat quiescent.

Gripped by wonder, she continued to toil up the slope towards the pass. The surface seemed to level out the higher she climbed. Kallis's face was blue, his tongue protruding. He would die soon, unless she could return him to the air.

The land shuddered. She was thrown onto her back and Kallis tumbled from her arms. She looked up.

For the first time in her life, the sun was sliding away from the zenith.

SHE LAY ON the shaking ground and watched the ball of light in the sky, fascinated. It moved smoothly, and ever more rapidly, dipping down towards the Edge mountains at the World's far rim—

No. The sun is still. It's the land that's moving, twisting about. And, as if in response, the earth roared in protest at this violation. The air was impossibly thin, but even so she could feel the winds plucking at her, whipping dust into her face as she tried to rise. She was riding the twisting land, she realised, as if it were some huge, stirring beast.

And now the sun touched the irregular rim of the mountains of the far Edge. For a moment the brilliant disc seemed to hover there; and then shadows, pools of the deepest black, swept across the hundreds of miles of land before her.

The sun disappeared. The light leaked from the sky.

She stood up, wondering. It was cold—she could feel it, but it didn't hurt her. A soft snow fell about her shoulders. But there were no clouds above her.

The snow is the air, she thought. The air is freezing.

And now, as her eyes adapted, she saw that the gathering darkness was not complete. Where the sun had been a single disc in the sky, she saw that a hundred—no, a thousand, a million—lesser lights speckled the blackening heavens, like flakes of ice. They are suns, she realised. Suns like our own, but so very far away.

Beside her, Kallis groaned. This cold, this lack of air, would kill him. She had to return him to the light. She bent, scooped him up, and, on her powerful new legs, carried him towards the pass in the World's Edge, a notch where beads of sunlight still played.

As the twist passed through the fabric of the World, the remote suns wheeled across the sky, and the deforming land shuddered beneath her feet.

SHE REACHED THE pass (it seemed to be artificial, a conduit on the rim of the World) and descended onto the light side. She entered a magical land: a land in which air and water hissed from the ground, billowing up at the touch of new sunlight.

She slithered down the 'slope' from the Edge, but paused before the hard undersurface disappeared beneath its covering of soil and dust. The air was thick enough here, but they were still so 'high', so far from the centre, that the land seemed tipped up. There would be floods, fires, more instabilities, she realised. It would be best to wait it out here.

The new landscape on this side of the World, devoid of water and life for generations, looked like a carved mask, with bare hills and empty valleys. She saw buildings, like the Scholars' tomb. So there were people here, too: more larvae who wouldn't become sunflies. Kallis would have company.

She wondered about the animals: the hornbeast, the sunflies. And the plants. Perhaps they had their own encysting mechanisms. Perhaps she would meet a Winter hornbeast, when she returned to the darkness.

Kallis stirred. Coughing, clutching at his chest, he struggled to his feet. Onara longed to run to him, to have his arms around her. But how might he react to seeing her in this new, monstrous guise?

She remained behind him as he stood and stared across the bowl of the landscape. "Onara," he gasped. "Are we still alive?"

She said gently, "I think there are people down there. See that cluster of buildings? There must be Scholars—or some equivalent—emerging from their long sleep. They must be as confused as you. I'm sure they'll welcome you. Go there, Kallis."

He turned to face her for the first time. His expression froze as he stared, horrified.

She held out her ugly hands. "Don't be afraid. I'm just—a sunfly. Don't you see?"

"Onara?"

She tried to find the words to explain to him. "I understand now. This is what encystment is for," she said. "Not so that a chosen few can hide out the Winter. But so that we can all—all of us—metamorphose into this new form, and ride the twisting World into darkness, survive to live a new life. Another phase of life."

The price of survival was to become monstrous: with a huge barrel chest, spindly legs, bloated arms... Like the Foe, she thought suddenly. I have become the Foe!

"You see how it must have been," she went on. "Once, all men became as I am. But there were some who resisted the change—like that sunfly larva we saw in the forest... And so they fought the Winter forms, their brothers. Dehumanised them."

Made them into monsters for children—made them into the Foe.

"And now we must live through this ghastly, perverted life, with a culling every thirty generations... But it was not meant to be like this, Kallis. We are meant to live in sunlight, and shadow..."

He stared at her, panting. Then, slowly, the fear subsided. He reached up towards her face. "Onara..."

She stumbled back from him, her new legs thick and awkward. "It's alright," she said. "I'm still Onara. But... but I can't stay with you." The air was like a clammy blanket around her; despite her ties to Kallis, she longed to be away from this damp, soft place, to return to the hard vacuum of the dark side.

Kallis stood. "Don't go. You'll be alone–"

"I have to go back, Kallis. The Winter is my world now. There is much that I must do."

She turned and ran towards the Edge. With her new, powerful legs, she scaled the formidable 'slope' as easily as she had scrambled up trees as a child.

She considered what lay ahead. Perhaps she might even return to her home—the Vale, the manse—all of it dead and destroyed now, a landscape of corpses, blanketed over by the frozen air.

She would find no life anywhere now—save in the Scholars' shelter...

She lifted her arms and, in awe, studied the muscles there. She could break into that shelter, let the vacuum enter and permit the encystment to take its full course. As it was meant to.

She thought of Almora, and Sch. Malken, and wondered how they might react to their metamorphoses.

She was the only sunfly in the world. But when she woke the Scholars, she would be alone no longer. She would bring to an end this huge cycle of repression and death.

When the Narrowing comes again, she thought, humans will be ready. All the people will survive the next turning. Become sunflies like me. I'll see to it.

She turned and looked down the 'slope'. Far below, Kallis was a small, dark figure, watching her. He saw her turn, and raised an arm in farewell. Onara lifted her misshapen arm, and waved.

Then she continued her ascent.

Winter awaited her: a new life, new goals. But she knew she would always keep her love for Kallis, like a warm, soft treasure, at the core of her being.

Within minutes she had reached the Edge of the World.

Stephen Baxter and Eric Brown

THE AUTHORS

STEPHEN BAXTER is the pre-eminent science-fiction writer of his generation. Published around the world, he has won major awards in the UK, US, Germany and Japan. Born in 1957, he has degrees from Cambridge and Southampton. His first short story was published in 1987, and his first novel, *Raft*, in 1991. He lives in Northumberland with his wife, and is the author of more than thirty books. His latest include the collection *Xeelee: Endurance*, and the novels *The Massacre of Mankind*, and *Xeelee: Vengeance*. His website can be found at:

www.stephen-baxter.com

ERIC BROWN has won the British Science Fiction Award twice for his short stories, and his novel *Helix Wars* was shortlisted for the 2012 Philip K Dick award. He has published over sixty books, and his latest include an SF novel *Binary System*, the crime novel *Murder Take Three*, and the novella *The Martian Simulacra*. He writes a regular science fiction review column for the *Guardian* newspaper and lives in Cockburnspath, Scotland. His website can be found at:

www.ericbrown.co.uk

ACKNOWLEDGEMENTS

'The Spacetime Pit' was first published in *Interzone 107*, May 1996.

'Green-Eyed Monster' was first published in *Spectrum SF #2*, April 2000.

'Sunfly' was first published in *Interzone 100*, October 1995.

Microcosms: Forty-Two stories
by Tony Ballantyne and Eric Brown
http://www.infinityplus.co.uk/book.php?book=ebtbmicro

Philip K Dick Award nominated writers Tony Ballantyne and Eric Brown bring together forty-two fantastical short-short stories, featuring new takes on every SF trope from alien invasion, robots, and time-travel, to stellar exploration, the future of computing, and the nature of the human soul.

Tony Ballantyne is the author of the acclaimed Penrose hard SF novels, *Twisted Metal* and *Blood and Iron*, as well as the groundbreaking and surreal fantasy novels *Dream London* and *Dream Paris*.

Eric Brown has written many SF and crime novels including *The Kings of Eternity*, *Kethani*, and *The Serene Invasion*.

Together they are a hundred years old.

'Eric Brown spins a terrific yarn.' – *SFX*

'This is as strange and unclassifiable a novel as it's possible to imagine, and a marvellous achievement.' – *Financial Times* on Tony Ballantyne's *Dream London*

'British writing with a deft, understated touch: wonderful.' – *New Scientist* on Eric Brown

'A new British star has arrived to join the likes of Hamilton, Reynolds and Banks.' – *Vector* on Tony Ballantyne

Parallax View
by Keith Brooke and Eric Brown
http://www.infinityplus.co.uk/book.php?book=kbrpv

'The stories in this collection are among the best science fiction. These are stories imbued with a rich intelligence and a deep sense of humanity. These are mature stories, tales of love and loss, of pleasure and pain. Cherish them.' – from the foreword by Stephen Baxter

Parallax View showcases 'In Transit', written specially for this collection, a novella set in a future war-torn universe in which human expansion has come up against the implacable Kryte. Xeno-psychologist Abbott finds himself the guardian of a deadly Kryte on a mission to study it on his return to Earth. When they crash-land on the fortress planet of St Jerome, the Kryte prisoner turns the tables and takes Abbott into terrible custody. What follows is a terrifying journey across a hellish landscape towards a finale that might change the destiny of the Kryte and humanity, forever…

Plus six other stories that examine the interface between human and alien – a parallax view from two of Britain's top science fiction writers, both shortlisted for the 2012 Philip K Dick Award.